MIDNIGHT ARCADE

Excellent Ernesto Cousins 3 / Wrestlevania

by Gabe Soria
art by Kendall Hale

Penguin Workshop

DIRECTIONS

One thing you'll learn quickly here is that it's not always easy to follow the instructions. You never know when the game . . . I mean, book . . . is going to send you to your doom. But if you want a truly exhilarating experience, you'll need to do exactly what the book tells you . . . except, of course, when you get to make a choice. In these cases, you should trust your gut.

When you see a game controller like the one below, you'll be presented with multiple options to move around or take an action. Once you make a choice, turn to the corresponding page and find the matching symbol.

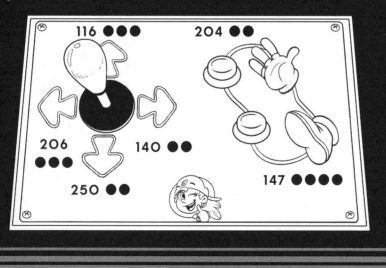

There can be as many as four sections on a page, so make sure you ONLY read the one marked with your symbol for that page.

At times, you'll be sent to a page and symbol without a choice or be presented with a chance to return to the previous stage. Do as you're instructed to keep the story flowing correctly.

Sometimes you'll make a wrong choice, and the game will end. At that time, you'll have a choice to either restart that level or exit the Midnight Arcade.

There are countless ways to read this book . . . I mean, play these games . . . I mean, read this book . . . I mean . . . Well, you get the picture. Have fun, and good luck!

Welcome to the

MIDNIGHT ARCADE

When your folks told you that you were going to be spending summer vacation at the beach, you couldn't contain your excitement. You spent the last couple of months of the school year fantasizing about sleeping late every day, then swimming all day, with breaks to take naps on the beach under an umbrella, maybe with a little surfing thrown in there for good measure, followed by watching horror movies on TV with a plate of nachos in your lap from sundown until you passed out on the couch. Yeah, those thoughts kept you going all through your final exams, and when school was finally out and you jumped into the back seat of the car for the long road trip that would take you to your personal beach paradise, you turned on some tunes, closed your eyes, and dreamed of the adventures that awaited you.

But your spirits dropped once you pulled off the highway and into the sleepy seaside village of San Retro Bay. It's not that your home for the next month is a *bad* place, it's just kind of . . . whatever. Sure, the town looks pretty neat and tidy, with all the vintage houses set symmetrically along the tree-lined streets that wind up and around the hills surrounding the bay, and the ice-cream shop on Main Street does have some pretty awesome sundaes, but other than that, San Retro Bay is, let's face it, kind of BORING and a bit weird. The beach is rocky and uninviting, the water's cold, and everybody in town is about a million years old. But you have to admit that there is at least one cool thing about the town: the San Retro Bay Boardwalk.

You found it one day when your family went for a drive to do something they called "antiquing." Claiming you couldn't go because of a stomach bug, you instead spent the day riding around town on the bike you brought, cruising the streets with no particular place to go. Eventually, your wanderings took you to downtown San Retro, the sleepy center of the town, and then down to the beach, and that's when you first spotted the partially rotted-out pier that ran parallel to the coastline. Attracted by the faint smell of corn dogs and the promise of thrill rides—you could see signs advertising a Ferris wheel and the wooden bones of a roller coaster in the distance—you locked up your bike and entered.

What you found was a sparsely populated row of commerce. You wandered up and down the quarter mile of food stands, souvenir shops, and ancient rides that had all seen better days. The Scare-Mansion haunted house, the bumper cars, and the Whiplash Coaster— the only cool-looking rides—were out of order, but the comic shop / used bookstore was neat (if a bit dusty), so you grabbed a couple of comics from the quarter bin and bought a corn dog with mustard (not bad, actually) and settled in on a bench to read.

That's when you heard it: Above the crashing of the waves behind you and the booming of the music soundtracking the spinning twist ride, you thought you heard the distinct chiming of digital sound effects, the type of stuff you only heard in OLD games.

You looked up to try to locate the source of the sound. Directly across from you, between the clam shack and the airbrush T-shirt stand, there was an arcade sitting smack in the middle of the boardwalk. You could have sworn that you hadn't seen it when you sat down, but there it was, plain as day. But from the looks of the boards over the windows and a handmade GAME OVER sign on the door, it hadn't been open in YEARS.

Curious, you stuck your comics in your back pocket and wandered over to the front of the arcade, trying to get a glimpse inside through the gaps in the boards. You thought you could make out the shadowy shapes of cabinets within, but it was so dark that you couldn't be sure. And then you realized that you weren't alone: Three kids—a beanpole of a boy with a backward baseball cap, a shorter girl wearing sunglasses, and an even smaller boy with a lollipop in his mouth—were standing next to you, each of them also trying to look inside. Locals, probably, and from the looks of it, siblings.

"It's haunted," the tall boy said.

"I heard some killer guy like in that movie lives there," said the girl. "They say you can hear him walking around in there at night."

"Aw, there ain't no killer guy. It's just raccoons," replied the littlest one, which prompted the girl to sock him on the shoulder. "Ow! I'm gonna tell Mom you keep hitting me!"

"Mom said stop hitting him!" barked the tall boy, socking his sister on the shoulder, which she accepted silently and then returned, punching her older brother back even harder and leaving him rubbing the spot.

"Jeez, why do you haveta hit so hard?" he said to his sister before remembering you were standing there. He gave you an appraising glance.

"Hey, kid, what are you up to?" he asked.

"Yeah, kid. You wanna hang out with us?" his sister added.

"I still say that it's GOTTA be raccoons!" the little brother said, prompting his sister to punch him in the shoulder again.

Shrugging and explaining you had no plans for the day, you followed the kids off the boardwalk, giving the storefront a last glance. *Gosh*, you thought. *How cool would it be if there was an ARCADE here?*

That was a few days ago, though, and you had practically forgotten about the arcade until a few minutes ago. You were peacefully crashed out on the couch when you heard it, that sound you last heard on the boardwalk, like an old video game, heard it so clearly that you looked around expecting to see someone playing a game next to you, but there was no one there. And then you heard it again, off in the distance. Before you knew what you were doing, you had checked to make sure everybody in the house was asleep before you quietly slipped out the door and hopped on to your bike, pedaling back toward downtown, following that sound almost as if you were hypnotized.

Now, once again, you're walking onto the San Retro Bay Boardwalk, and if it was a weird place during the day, at night it's downright spooky and desolate. The lights of the streetlamps (the ones that aren't burnt-out entirely, that is) are flickering ominously, and the only thing you can hear is the rhythmic rolling of the ocean.

But wait. That's actually not true. You CAN hear something—you can hear the sounds of games like you heard before, but they're louder now, and they're coming from somewhere farther down the boardwalk. You must, of course, investigate, so you begin creeping toward the source of the noise.

Moments later, you're in front of the old arcade, and though the place is still closed up tight, SOMETHING is happening inside. Colored light spills out from the gaps between the boards on the windows, and now the glorious sound of video game music and sound effects is even louder. *What's going on?* you wonder. And then you notice that the boards that were holding the gate closed earlier this week have been removed by someone . . . or some*thing*. Your curiosity gets the better of you, and before you realize what you're doing, you've pulled the creaking gate aside and turned the knob on the door to enter, whereupon you are immediately engulfed in a cloud of billowing smoke and faint light . . .

. . . and find yourself inside a fully functional, completely electrified, honest-to-goodness ARCADE. The place itself is dimly lit—there are no overhead lights on—but the interior of the arcade is glowing nevertheless, an eerily beautiful rainbow of reds, greens, blues, and yellows emanating from video screens contained in old-style wooden cabinets. Amazed, you begin to wander through the interior of the arcade, which feels somehow . . . bigger on the inside than it looked on the outside. There are hundreds of games inside its mazelike interior, and you recognize the names of some of them, but many of them are unfamiliar to you—*Crypt Quest? Space Battles? MowTown?* Never heard of 'em. But they sure LOOK cool. And the sound that surrounds you, the glorious cacophony of lasers being fired, enemies being slayed, power-ups being grabbed, special weapons being deployed, and tinny soundtracks being played, is like the most excellent symphony you've ever heard. Better than Mozart, anyway.

But when you round a corner made by two cabinets

with the titles *Gofer* and *Tuff Beatdown* emblazoned on their sides, two more games you've never heard of, a chill runs down your spine and then throughout your entire body: You're not alone here. At the end of the aisle, there's a young man! His hair is shaggy and falls to his shoulders, and he's dressed in faded jeans and a two-toned baseball-style T-shirt. But his back is to you, and you quickly duck behind one of the arcade games before he sees you. There's someone here—and you've broken in! Fear rises in your stomach, and you know that you have to get out before you're discovered.

You back up slowwwwwwly, like a character in one of those old cartoons that your dad likes, then turn to finish sneaking out, hoping that you can find your way to the exit while crouch-running. You're on the right track, only to find the person you just saw now standing directly in front of you. But . . . how? How did he move so FAST? You begin to stammer out an apology, trying out multiple excuses as to why you're inside, the words tripping off your tongue before you can even think about them. Something about being lost, and then having amnesia and being a foreign exchange student who can't read

Keep Out signs. Nonsense, all of it, and you expect the guy in front of you to grab you at any moment and threaten to call the cops, but he doesn't. Instead, he smiles.

"Far OUT," says the mysterious dude, practically grinning now. He raises an eyebrow. "Say . . ." The dude reaches behind his back and pulls a tray of chips covered with melted cheese, beans, onions, and sour cream out of nowhere, like a magician. "You wouldn't by any chance dig some nachos, would you?"

Hesitantly (and hungrily), you reach out for a chip and gingerly put it in your mouth. You wait a moment, wondering if you should eat nachos offered by a stranger, but you think being polite might keep you out of trouble, so you grab the tray and begin to scarf them down. They're basically the greatest nachos you've EVER had.

"Aren't those basically the greatest nachos you've ever had?" the dude asks. You nod eagerly, your mouth still full of chips. "Follow me," he says as he brushes past you and begins walking through the maze of games. After a few steps he notices that you aren't following and stops. Turning around, he spreads his arms. "Oh, sorry: Welcome to this palace of mysterious digital delights. Welcome to the Midnight Arcade!" It's only now that you notice the logo of the Midnight Arcade emblazoned across his chest and a change-making device on a belt around his waist. "Oh, hey— dig this . . ." He reaches down to the change machine on his belt and operates one of the levers on the side, which shoots something shiny into his hand, which he tosses to you. You catch the object on the fly, and opening your palm, you realize that it's a coin—but unlike any you've ever seen before.

It's a token! Just like the ones you used to get at Pete's Pizza Party Fun Place when you were a kid to play skee-ball, air hockey, and video games. But this token is different from the ones you used to get at birthday parties past; this one feels . . . well, as strange as it seems even thinking it, the token feels like there's some sort of bizarre ENERGY emanating from it, vibrating, almost magical. But that's silly, isn't it?

Isn't it?

"You're gonna need that where we're going. Follow me," he says mysteriously as he resumes walking away.

Figuring that someone who makes such great nachos deserves the benefit of the doubt (and knowing that you've got nothing better to do), you shrug and catch up.

❖ ❖ ❖

The arcade attendant leads you deeper into the Midnight Arcade, and the farther you get, the more blown away you are by how BIG it is; it must be the size of a football field inside. How is that even possible? You also notice that a strange kind of fog is creeping out from between the cabinets, hovering just above the carpeted floor, adding to the eerie vibe.

"Lots of cool games here at the Midnight Arcade," the attendant says. "You might recognize some of them, and others . . . well, let's just say that some items in our collection are rarer than rare."

As the attendant chatters on, you pass an intersection of game avenues, and you glance off to one side: You don't know why, but you're suddenly convinced that there's something cool down that way. You can feel it. Wandering off in that direction and away from the attendant, you find yourself down a short alley of games that dead-ends in a cul-de-sac where two game cabinets sit side by side. The fog here is so thick, the machines look like they're practically floating on neon clouds.

"Hey, nice instincts!" says the attendant, who emerges out of the fog between the two machines. But . . . wasn't he BEHIND you? And isn't this a dead end? How . . . ? He spreads his arms and puts a hand on the top of each game, like a proud salesman displaying his wares. "You found two of the coolest games here."

Each game has its own unique appeal: You've actually played the original *Excellent Ernesto Cousins* and *Excellent Ernesto Cousins 2*, but the third game in the series . . . it's an urban myth! NOBODY'S played it, and the rumor you heard was that it was too weird to be released. All copies of it were supposed to have been destroyed! And *Wrestlevania*'s grappling creatures look pretty awesome and intense, and whatever the game actually is, it's probably scary and wild.

"That token must be burning a hole in your pocket,"

the attendant says, and he's right: It actually feels WARM in there, possibly from the vibrations. You pull it out and hold it in your hand. "So why don'tcha USE it, eh? These games aren't going to play themselves."

You nod, and holding the token tightly between thumb and forefinger, you walk forward.

If you want to play *Wrestlevania*, head to 126 ●●●●

If you want to play *Excellent Ernesto Cousins 3*, head to 75 ●●●●

●

Frankenwrestler gets closer, and when it's almost upon you, you jump up and extend both of your legs, driving them directly into the monster's chest. The impact forces you both to fall to the mat, stunned! You crawl away, as does Frankenwrestler, and each of you retreats to a corner, both being careful not to touch the sides of the cage. It gets to its feet, shakes both of its heads, and moans in anger. Then it runs at you again. Try another move!

Head back to 33 ●●

●●

You notice a large button on the dashboard of the car, and you decide to press it. When you do, a spinning buzz saw blade shoots from the grille of the car, zooming over the surface of the road before dropping to the ground and shooting off sparks as it rolls off the road and into the distance. Cool! Test out the other controls or . . .

To test out the other controls,
head back to 182 ●●●

To continue on, head to 150 ●●

EXCELLENT ERNESTO EXPLAINS

You lay the only coin you found into the tray and push in the plunger with a satisfying CHUNK. The Ernesto automaton immediately comes to life and begins to gab.

"One coin, eh? That's it? Okay, here goes: Long ago, my cousin and I came to this land, the Dandelion Kingdom, and had many adventures, saving princesses and princes and, in the process, saving the land itself. Then we'd come back and do it all again, slightly the same way, but with a little variation. It was fun, sure, but after a few times, it kind of became like a job, and we already had good jobs as carpenters . . ."

The machine's eyes rapidly blink a few times, and its head shakes back and forth as it makes a sound that almost makes you think something's gone wrong inside. It stops talking entirely for a few seconds, then abruptly comes back to life.

"Sorry, sorry. It's been a long time since anybody's used me. Anyway, that's all of the story you get for one coin. Sorry to leave you hanging!" The automaton's eyes close, and no matter how many times you bang on the glass, it won't start talking again. Argh! And then to top everything off, you feel your body start to dematerialize.

If you want to play _Wrestlevania_ now, head to 126 ●●●●

If you've beaten this game and _Wrestlevania_, head to 265 ●●●●

If you want to play again later, come back anytime. You have infinite continues!

●●●●

You bump into the smooth walls of the stone hallway. They're damp with humidity, but there's nothing more to them.

Head back to 141 ●●●●

●

You push backward with your feet, taking Dracula off guard! You both stumble back, into a turnbuckle, and the force of the impact makes Dracula lose his hold on you! Shaking him off, you hustle back to the center of the ring and turn to face your enemy. Good one, Champ!

Head to 169 ●●●●

●●

Your wooden car is still hurtling along the road to Ernestopia, and the two other cars, the ones driven by the weird Excellent Ernesto Cousin's puppets, are both ahead of you, one in your lane and the other in the lane to your left. What do you do?

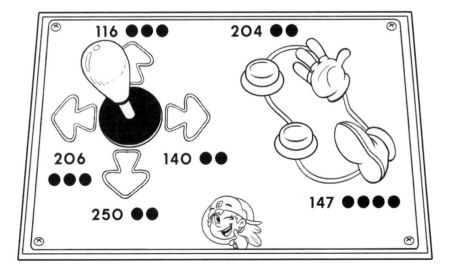

You leap into the air and come down with your elbow crooked, ready to deliver a crushing blow to an opponent, but there's nobody there. You have defeated the floor. Congratulations! That's good wrestling practice. Now make another choice.

Head back to 58 ●●●●

For some reason, you decide to go back in the direction from which you just came. Maybe the door to Dracula's study will be unlocked now. Who knows? Soon, the paintings are behind you and you see something ahead in the chandelier-lit hallway. A few moments later you're somehow back in front of the paintings. What? You'd better pick again.

Head back to 66 ●●●

You've taken the lead and are now once again ahead of the Ernesto puppet's car and rocketing toward Ernestopia, which is getting closer with every passing second. You're almost at the finish line, but that's when the other car pulls over into the middle lane—YOUR lane—and begins to gain ground. Not only that, you see that its front grille has opened up, and inside you notice the gleam of a buzz saw blade. They're armed just like you are, of course! The buzz saw stays there for only a second, though; the next moment it's launched directly at you! Maneuver: now!

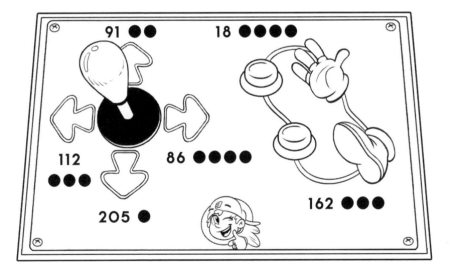

91 ●●   18 ●●●●

112
●●●   86 ●●●●

205 ●   162 ●●●

● ●

You figure that this is the perfect chance to give the audience a real show by humiliating their lord and master, so you stroll over to Dracula and give him a quick ONE! TWO! THREE! stomps on his undead head. The crowd yells at you.

"Bum!"

"Cheater!"

"Kill the mortal!"

But you LOVE it. Walking to the ropes, you cup your hand to your ear in the universal "Monster audience says what?" gesture, and it drives them even more insane! Bring it on! But you're a professional, and it's time to finish this monster business, so you turn back to Dracula . . . only to find him standing . . . and mad!

"Silly Champ, you should haff put a stake in me vhen you had the chance. Now, ve fight more!"

Head back to 70 ● ● ● ●

● ● ●

Nothing there but a barrier made out of stone and some sort of algae. Your choices seem to be going forward or back to the surface. Play another way.

Head back to 231 ●

●●●●

You halt your forward movement in the presence of the Noctopus and do an about-face, hoping to flee from its arms and retreat, maybe try to make it back to the surface. Unfortunately, you simply can't run fast enough, and before you can even make it a few feet, the Noctopus's tentacles reach out and grab you by the legs, pulling you toward its creepy eyebrows and chomping mouth . . .

YOU ARE DEAD. CONTINUE: Y/N?
Y: Head to 132 ●●●   **N:** Head to 265 ●●●●

●

For some reason you think that using one of your patented wrestling moves right now is a good idea. Contrary to your opinion, it's not, and the time you just wasted has proved to be your undoing as another chandelier falls directly on top of you.

YOU ARE DEAD. CONTINUE: Y/N?
Y: Head to 20 ●●   **N:** Head to 265 ●●●●

Holding the line, you drive your wooden car directly into the huge chasm, falling down the side of the cliff and causing the car to explode in a shower of sawdust. It's safe to say that you're not getting your learner's permit anytime soon because . . .

YOU ARE DEAD. CONTINUE: Y/N?
Y: Head to 23 ●● N: Head to 265 ●●●●

●●●

The more you struggle, the tighter Dracula's grip gets. It's like he's turned into an anaconda instead of a bat! He squeezes you tighter . . . tighter . . . tighter . . . and then *POP!* (We'll leave it to your imagination which body part— or parts—of yours is no longer attached. All the same . . .)

YOU ARE DEAD. CONTINUE: Y/N?
Y: Head to 34 ●●●● N: Head to 265 ●●●●

●●●●

You dodge to the left and avoid Frankenwrestler's mad dash, smacking it on its heads as it passes. That only serves to make it madder, and it twirls around and runs at you again. You'll have to try another move!

Head back to 33 ●●

Wait—it's a spider, it's on the floor, and you're the CHAMP. What else can you do but step on the thing? Of course! You raise your leg and—imagining that the spider is an opponent lying helpless within the ring after a particularly effective bulldog—bring your foot down on the spider, crushing it and sending arachnid goo splattering everywhere. *SPLAT.* You're disgusted but happy to be alive and to have invented a new wrestling move, something you're thinking of calling "The Spider Stomp."

But your satisfaction at your creation is short-lived, for you notice that something else is coming up the stairs . . . another spider, and another, and another! And if giant spiders could be angry, you'd swear they were FURIOUS. It's time to leave, and you continue to race up the stairs, pursued by a bloodthirsty pack of eight-legged creatures!

Head to 62 ●

No matter which way you move, you can't break free of Dracula's terrible hold. The vampire is just too strong for you to overpower him with brute force! You'll have to use his own power against him, but that will have to be the next time you play, for the King of Vampires is now sinking his sharp canines into your flesh and sucking your lifeblood out of you! Welp . . .

YOU ARE DEAD. CONTINUE: Y/N?
Y: Head to 34 ●●●● N: Head to 265 ●●●●

●●●

The crab-like creature viciously snaps its claws and jaws at you, protecting whatever is inside the chest. It's time to fight!

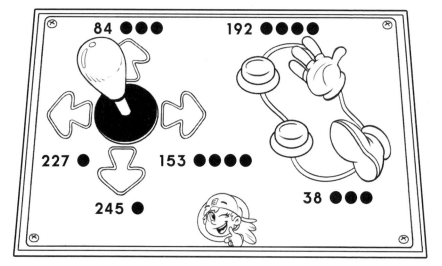

●●●●

You jam your foot down on the accelerator, which turns out not to be the best of plans, as it brings your wheels into contact with the nails that much sooner. The tiny pieces of metal shred your front wheels into toothpicks and send your car flying end over end and then smashing it, and you, into Popsicle sticks on the road.

YOU ARE DEAD. CONTINUE: Y/N?
Y: Head to 150 ●● N: Head to 265 ●●●●

●

You back away from Dracula as he hurtles toward you, clawed hands reaching for your neck! You try to defend yourself, but he's too quick for you and knocks you down to the mat, slashing at you in what surely must be a violation of the rules, finally finishing you off with a hearty bite to the neck. You almost made it, but almost doesn't cut it in . . . *WRESTLEVANIA!*

YOU ARE DEAD. CONTINUE: Y/N?
Y: Head to 169 ●●●● N: Head to 265 ●●●●

••

You and El Hombre Lobo are locked in a grapple, and your opponent growls menacingly in your face. You recognize that this is the call of the wild . . . the call to wrestle! What's your next move?

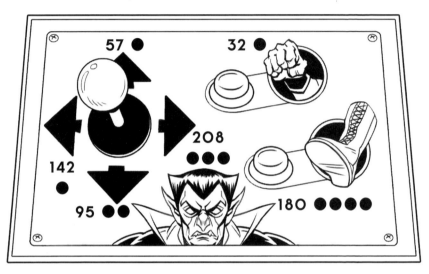

●●●

You back up, and Dracula practically FLIES at you, so quickly, it looks like he's turned partly into mist. Shocked, you aren't ready for it when he leaps at you with both feet and kicks you in the chest, driving you into and OVER the ropes! You fall outside the ring, in the process slamming your head on the ground so hard, you can't see straight. Bell fully rung, you struggle to get to your feet, and you look up just in time to see Dracula jumping from the turnbuckle, arms spread, mouth wide, and fangs extended, directly at you! Before you can react, his teeth are buried in your neck, and . . .

YOU ARE DEAD. CONTINUE: Y/N?
Y: Head to 70 ●●●● N: Head to 265 ●●●●

●●●●

You continue straight ahead, hoping that your car can crash through the wooden barrier. Your hopes, however, are misplaced, and you crash—*BOOM!*—into the gate to Ernestopia, barely making a crack in it. That's it, my friend.

YOU ARE DEAD. CONTINUE: Y/N?
Y: Head to 238 ● N: Head to 265 ●●●●

You've bonked the Noctopus on the head and saved yourself from certain doom, but another alert from your air gauge tells you that you've either wasted too much time or spent too much energy so far, because now you're down to three units of breathing time. You'd better hustle.

And that's when you see it—off to your left there is what appears to be an ornate wooden chest, like the kind that pirates hide their treasure in. Off to your right rests *another* chest that looks exactly like the first one. There might be something cool in them, or they might contain some sort of monster like the chest in the beach hut, or even worse, be empty and a waste of time . . . and air. What's your next move?

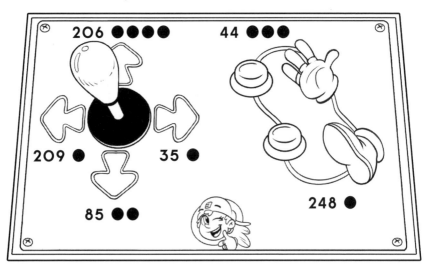

Delving deeper into the network of sewer tunnels beneath the Groovy Gardens, you follow the corridor along its twisty, wet way, slipping occasionally on the slick surface, even ending up with your butt in the water not once, but twice. All the while, the frog sound becomes louder, scarier. Soon, however, you come to a crossroads of a sort; another pipe and ladder lead upward, to the surface, at the top of which you can see the fitful, pale sunshine of the world above. The tunnel, however, branches off, and you can hear the frog sound echoing toward you from deeper in the network of tunnels. Where do you go?

If you decide to climb up the ladder and go back to the surface, head to 254 ●●

If you decide to continue to explore the tunnel, head to 212 ●

● ● ●

The only thing that way is cold, hard castle wall, which as of yet you are not able to break through! The chandelier above is swinging crazily and will fall any second, so the time to decide on another action is now!

Head back to 125 ●●

You think quickly and press the button for your weapon, and the buzz saw flies away from your car but has nothing to connect with. You'll have to think of something else!

Head back to 7 ●

●

You move away from Frankenwrestler's body, for some reason deciding not to press your advantage. That proves to be a mistake, for moments later it rouses itself and stands up, ready once again to wrestle.

It takes a swing at you, and you manage to dodge. But not for long . . .

Head to 33 ●●

●●

You pull the wheel to the left and whip your car around the hardware obstacle in the road. Good thinking!

Head to 5 ●●

● ● ●

Moving against the water, you continue forward along the undersea path. Looking down at your air gauge, you see that you have only five units left. Better hurry!

Head to 132 ● ● ●

● ● ● ●

You walk up to the rattled werewolf and stomp on him once, hard and without mercy. This is wrestling, after all—THE REAL DEAL. The creature howls in pain, literally, and writhes around on the mat. Pick another action!

Head back to 199 ●

●

You decide to fight back, so you turn your wheel to the right. This takes the Ernesto puppet driving the other car by surprise, and they lose control of their vehicle and spin out, allowing you to take the lead. Rad.

Head to 7 ●

The grime wiped away, you can now see that each painting has a title, beneath which are cryptic symbols. They read:

Silver Bullet

Torch and Pitchfork

Wooden Stake

Huh. If you didn't know better, you'd think the paintings were trying to tell you how to play the game.

Suddenly the breeze you felt before begins to get stronger, more powerful, causing the chandeliers above to sway, gently at first, but then the wind picks up and sets them to swinging wildly. And then . . . *SNAP!* The chandelier behind you breaks its chain and falls to the ground, igniting into a fireball that blocks the path back. You can't go back, and from the looks of it, the chandeliers ahead are about to fall, too!

Think fast!

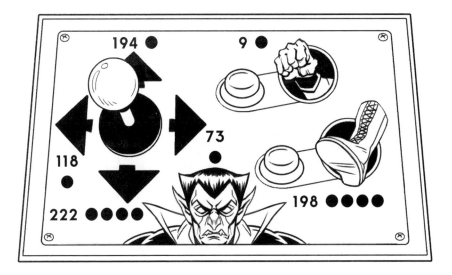

●●●

You jam your foot down on the gas pedal, and your car zooms forward with a thrilling burst of speed. You ease up on it, and your car returns to its cruising speed. Test out the other controls or . . .

To test out the other controls, head back to 182 ●●●

To continue on, head to 150 ●●

Thinking that speed is the key to escaping from this predicament, you accelerate. Unfortunately, you and the other car are locked together at the wheels, and your sudden burst of energy causes the both of you to lose control and start spinning together like a weird top made out of two wooden cars, finally twirling into the side of the road and flying apart like a pile of sticks. Face it, cousin . . .

YOU ARE DEAD. CONTINUE: Y/N?
Y: Head to 185 ●●●● N: Head to 265 ●●●●

●

The assembled undead yahoos begin to climb over the barrier separating them from you, so you back away from them . . . and back right into the crowd of assembled undead yahoos on the OTHER side! Together, they form a ring around you, seething with a fan's animosity toward the challenger to the local champ . . . and then they close in! Too bad, Champ . . .

YOU ARE DEAD. CONTINUE: Y/N?
Y: Head to 154 ●● N: Head to 265 ●●●●

●●

You've eliminated one of your competitors, but one of them is still on the track, racing ahead of you. Large hills rise on either side of the road, sealing you in. Suddenly the Ernesto puppet car crosses both lanes, ending up all the way on the right, and a second later you can see why—there's an enormous pothole gouged into the left and center lanes, a rut in the blacktop so deep and wide, it's more like a pot-CANYON than a pothole, and you're coming up on it rapidly. But then you also notice something else: On the left-hand side of the road there appears to be a cleverly disguised tunnel cut into the side of the hill. What's your next move?

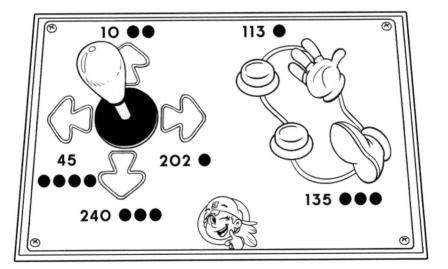

●●●

You twist your body to the left, and all that does is send you spinning aimlessly as you continue to fall toward the mountains below. Think of something else . . . quick!

Head back to 222 ●

●●●●

You can't go that way. There's nothing but wet sewer wall with thick roots that seem to move as you look at them. But there's nowhere to go. Choose another direction.

Head back to 231 ●

●

You roll to the right just as Frankenwrestler tosses the slab right where you just were, and the piece of lab furniture smashes into pieces outside the ring. That was good thinking, but you'll have to do better if you want to win this match.

Head to 33 ●●

●●

"Vun!" echoes a booming, disembodied voice from somewhere beyond the ring, a voice that you recognize.

El Hombre Lobo struggles weakly against you, but you persist in holding the beast down no matter how much he snarls.

"Two!" the voice continues. This count is counting!

Your opponent snaps his jaws at you, trying to get you to release your hold that's preventing you from being bitten and cursed with lycanthropy, but none of his attempts manage to break your skin.

"Three!" the voice concludes with a flourish, and on that count of three, thunder rumbles in the sky and a bolt of lightning crackles down from the heavens and strikes the middle of the ring, tossing you and El Hombre Lobo to opposite corners. Both of your bodies are smoking, but strangely, you are completely unhurt. A moment passes as you collect your thoughts, and then you slowly pull yourself to your feet while El Hombre Lobo stays down. You raise your hands above your head—no one was watching the match, but you have WON. You are still the CHAMPION.

Or you THOUGHT that no one was watching, for in the darkness of the woods beyond the ring you hear . . .

the sound of clapping. Someone out there is giving you a round of slow applause! After a moment, that someone emerges from the shadows, and you see the face of your one-person audience . . . DRACULA!

"A rousing victory, Champ. You haff done vell against your first challenge. But I vonder how vill you fare against your next . . ."—the vampire chuckles evilly during his dramatic pause—"opponent? Or should I say . . . opponents?" The grim chuckle turns into a full-throated, villainous laugh. "I suppose that my qvestion shall be answered soon. Find your next match, and if you survive it, find ME!"

Dracula's cape swirls around him as his form twists once again, in the blink of an eye transforming into a bat! You try to grab the undead flying mammal, but it's too swift for you and rises into the air, flapping its wings. You flex your muscles in anger, and as you do, you hear the sound of coughing behind you. Turning, you see that your opponent is recovering and slowly raising himself from the floor. You tense up, expecting a rematch, but you see that El Hombre Lobo is changing again, this time from werewolf back to his human form. He beckons to you, and you rush to his side.

"You have defeated me and, I think, defeated my curse.

At least for a moment," he says. "*Lo siento*, but I regret to say that I am too weak to join you in your quest to defeat *el vampiro*. I wish you . . . *buena suerte*! Ughhh . . ."

El Hombre Lobo's eyes close, but a quick check reveals that he's still breathing. Being turned into a werewolf and losing the match must have depleted his energy. Gently, you lay him back down on the ground. Then you stand to face the castle in the distance, and you see that once again, storm clouds are gathering, swirling over the fearsome structure in what can only be a video gaming omen meant to point you in the direction of your next match. You scowl grimly and point a challenging finger at the edifice of brick and stone in the distance. You don't know exactly how you're going to get out of this game and return home, but you're beginning to figure it out. There's probably one thing and one thing only that'll get the job done:

DRACULA. MUST. BE. SUPLEXED!

The match against El Hombre Lobo over, you pause for a moment to catch your breath and take stock of the situation, checking bullet points of weird information in your brain:

- You are trapped in a wrestling video game.
- Your friend and colleague has been turned into a bloodthirsty, wrestling werewolf, whom you have defeated.
- Your other friends, the tag team of Boris and Elsa, are still missing and probably in need of help.
- And somewhere out there, Dracula is waiting for you, hungry for your blood . . . and your CHAMPIONSHIP BELT.
- YOU ARE TRAPPED IN A WRESTLING VIDEO GAME.

You touch your belt again to reassure yourself of its presence, and as you do, you can hear the sound of a spooky organ playing somewhere in the distance. Its dissonant tones raise goose bumps on your flesh.

You can still hear the beating wings of the bat that is Dracula, and his voice, magically amplified, cries out:

"Vell done, Champ. You have defeated the first

adversary of the evening, but can you survive the rest of the frightening fights ahead of you? Find your next . . . opponent, and if you manage to best them, then you shall face me. But I varn you—your next match is a DOUBLEHEADER. Ah-ha-ha-ha!"

You think about his words: What could they mean? Finding the next match is pretty self-explanatory, but . . . a doubleheader? It's a puzzle, but as your wise old trainer used to say, you'll climb through those ropes when you get to that ring.

Lightning strikes again, close, and you look up to see the castle of Dracula wreathed in electricity; a dark cloud sits above the sinister structure, from which bolts of energy emanate, dancing around the parapets and turrets of the terrifying edifice. They seem, however, to be drawn to one tower in particular, almost as if something were attracting the infernal arcs of energy toward it and bending the fury of the heavens to someone's evil will. Squinting, you can see that a kite is tethered to the tower, and it's attracting the fiery bolts. And there's something else. You can't quite make it out, but there seems to be some sort of platform up there, exposed to the elements. As you watch, the platform slowly lowers until it disappears from view.

What could it possibly mean?

Whatever secret it holds, you know that the tower is calling to you. Perhaps it's the surplus of static electricity in the air, but your muscles twitch in anticipation of a new conflict, and upon witnessing this awesome and frightening display, you know that your next destination MUST be at the top of Dracula's castle. You kneel to check the vital signs of El Hombre Lobo: He's unconscious and his breathing is shallow, but he *is* breathing. Your Silver Bullet finishing move has driven the curse of lycanthropy from him—at least for now. Satisfied, you know it's time to move. The path to the castle is ahead of you and the haunted forest is to your right, left, and behind you.

What's your next move?

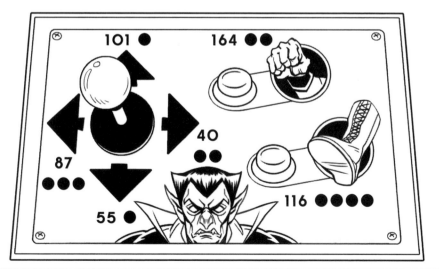

●●●

You try to move forward through the mass of Dandies, but they're too numerous and won't let you pass.

Trying to stay calm, you wonder what must be going on in the world outside the Midnight Arcade. Surely your family will start to worry if you don't return soon. Will they call the San Retro Bay Police and file a missing persons report? Would anyone else be able to find you in this game, even if they did search the boarded-up building? But you don't have to worry about all that right now.

Try a different action.

Head back to 75 ●●●●

You scream a war cry as you rush toward the Noctopus, foolishly hoping that your charge will scare it back into the ocean. And yes, "foolishly" is the correct word, for if the creature could smile, you'd swear it does as its tentacles wrap around your legs and it retreats back into its watery lair.

No problem, you think. *I've still got the diving suit on.* Then you remember: *Oh yes, the helmet. It's back on the beach. Aha.* Well, the Noctopus will get you if the water doesn't first, but either way . . .

YOU ARE DEAD. CONTINUE: Y/N?
Y: Head to 39 ● N: Head to 265 ●●●●

●

You break your hold on El Hombre Lobo and try to stun him with a cross chop, but the wrasslin' werewolf is unimpressed! Raising his clawed hands, he retaliates with a devastating double-slash, and . . .

YOU ARE DEAD. CONTINUE: Y/N?
Y: Head to 14 ●● N: Head to 265 ●●●●

Enraged that you've avoided its attack, Frankenwrestler howls in rage and CHARGES directly toward you! What's your next move?

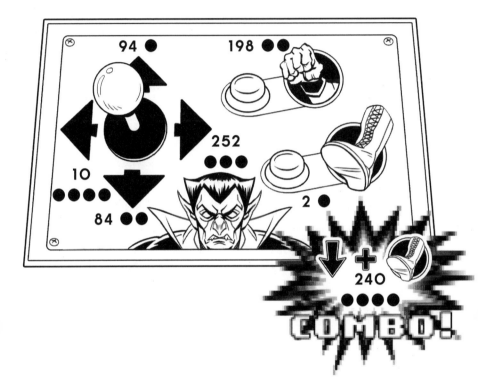

●●●

You try to brake, but you're going too fast, and you smack right into the closed gate, breaking your wooden car (and, er, you) into firewood. Too bad, kid.

YOU ARE DEAD. CONTINUE: Y/N?
Y: Head to 238 ● N: Head to 265 ●●●●

●●●●

Stunned an easy move worked, you taunt the audience, flexing your muscles. This makes the undead truly come alive! While you're playing around, Dracula snares you in a choke hold! What's your next move?

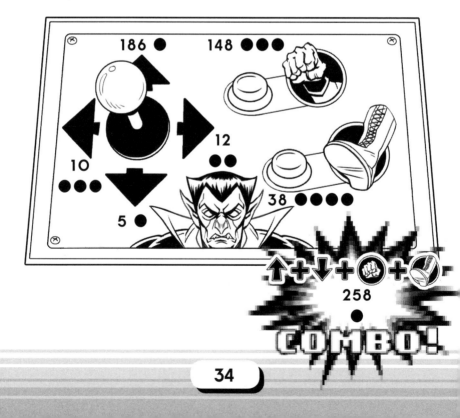

You pull off the main path and go to the treasure chest on the right. When you get close, you can see that there is a large lock keeping the lid sealed. You pull on the lock, hoping that maybe years of being on the bottom of the Serendipity Sea have weakened it somewhat, but that's not the case. It's shut tight, and no amount of your intense struggle works.

And that's when the frantic beeping starts—you look at your gauge and see that it's reading empty—you're out of air! Hoping that you can stave off the inevitable, you leave the chest behind and make a break for it, but in your panic, you head off in an unfamiliar direction and get lost among the kelp. You frantically look for a way out, but you're out of options and out of air! Sorry, cousin . . .

YOU ARE DEAD. CONTINUE: Y/N?
Y: Head to 16 ● N: Head to 265 ●●●●

●●

As you get closer to the blocked part of the pathway, you gather up all your strength and . . . LEAP, hoping to make it OVER the barrier. Sadly, though, you don't even get close to clearing the high jump, instead colliding painfully with the dense wood and falling back to the path. Stunned, you barely notice as the Stormy passes over you. Tsk, tsk . . .

YOU ARE DEAD. CONTINUE: Y/N?
Y: Head to 119 ●● N: Head to 265 ●●●●

●●●

What are you? Some amateur wrestler in a backyard league? Why would you back away from an opponent so close to defeat? Well, that move is going to cost you, for Dracula places his arms behind his head and tumbles backward, rolling until he's upright again! He claps his hands together and then gestures with his fingers in the universal signal for "Come get me, mortal fool."

Yes, he means you. You're the mortal fool.

Head back to 70 ●●●●

●●●●

You decide to meet Dracula's charge head-on and run right at him, but he leaps over you with vampiric agility, kicking you in the back for good measure as he vaults over you. You lose your balance and fall to your knees. Dracula swoops back toward you and knocks you down with a Flying Transylvanian Bat Battering Ram! Brutal! Dracula stands over you, his boot on your back, as the hunchback counts it off. "One . . . two . . . three!" The sound in the crypt arena is so deafening, you'd think they were having some sort of mad, monstrous PARTY. You feel yourself being lifted up into the air, over Dracula's head, and then THROWN into the crowd! That's that. You've lost the match, and . . .

YOU ARE DEAD. CONTINUE: Y/N?
Y: Head to 169 ●●●● N: Head to 265 ●●●●

●

You begin to circle to the left, looking for a weakness to exploit, and El Hombre Lobo mirrors your action, moving in a hunched-over, bestial manner, his claws ready to strike. But he doesn't . . . not yet. It seems as if he's waiting for you to make the first move. Pick another tactic.

Head back to 171 ●●●

●●

As the chandelier begins to fall, you decide to take it out, wrestling-style, with a dropkick. Your foot shatters the falling object, clearing the way in front of you.

Head to 63 ●●●

●●●

You leap up into the air—*SPROING!*—just as the crab creature rushes forward. Hanging for a moment, thanks to the strange gravity of the Dandelion Kingdom, you come down directly on top of the crab creature's carapace and lose your footing, stumbling to the ground but flipping the creature over in the bargain, exposing its fleshy stomach in the process. You've incapacitated it . . . for now!

Head to 104 ●●

●●●●

Bouncing up and down, you try to lift Dracula from the mat. Kicking your feet, you try to strike him in a vulnerable spot (surely vampires must not like it when you step on their toes?). Either way, this doesn't seem to be working, and you are rapidly running out of oxygen. Think of something else!

Head back to 34 ●●●●

You crawl onto the beach of the island, taking off your diving helmet and tossing it aside, swallowing great gulps of air, happy to have survived your crossing of the bottom of the Serendipity Sea. The sun is finally going down, and it sets the surface of the sea ablaze with glorious color. Wow. You've gotta admit it—it's pretty cool.

But your rest and reverie is short-lived, for you see something else emerge from the ocean. The Noctopus has followed you to the sandy shore, pulling itself from the waves on its inky-black tentacles, its toothy-beaky mouth open to gobble you up, its eyes alight with hunger! (Well, one of them, at least. Your speargun bolt is still embedded in its other eye.) You'd better think fast!

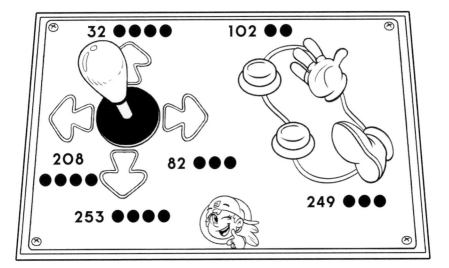

●●

You go to the right and attempt to leave the ring that way, but the roots and branches of the spooky trees of the forest bar your way. There is no exit in this direction.

Head back to 25 ●●

You brake, but the other car brakes with you and continues to push you to the side. You need to break free somehow. Pick another tactic.

Head back to 185 ●●●●

●●●●

You lunge forward and clip Dracula with an elbow, taking the vampire by surprise and causing him to stumble backward into the ropes. Good one, Champ! But he recovers quickly and comes back at you. You're back where you started. What—you thought the match was going to be decided this early? C'mon! Try again.

Head back to 70 ●●●●

You jump up—*SPROING!*—and land with a satisfying thud on top of the paving stone you were standing on, and as you do, you feel the stone begin to VIBRATE beneath your feet. Wary that it's some sort of trap, you jump back. And just in time, too, for as you do, the stone also begins to GLOW brightly. Then, the stone pulls itself up from the garden floor and hovers there, a full foot of space between it and the ground. But it's not finished—the stone then becomes another stone, and that stone becomes another stone, and on and on until the floating stones have formed an ascending staircase of platforms leading up and over the Groovy Gardens. That's pretty, uh, groovy!

But that's not all that's been revealed, for now there is a hole where the stone was, a deep well that descends into darkness. A metal ladder leads down into the inky black, and you can't see the bottom.

Do you trot up the platforms and see where they take you or climb down the ladder and see what's going on in the Groovy Gardens drainage system?

If you ascend the platform stone staircase, head to 242 ●●●●

If you decide to descend into the drainage pipe, go to 81 ●

You back away from the crowd of Dandies in front of you, but they're behind you, as well, and are blocking your way. Do something else.

Head back to 75 ●●●●

●●●

There's just a slimy wall there, dripping with water. You touch it with your fingertips and look at the goo that now covers part of your glove. But there's nowhere to go. Choose another direction.

Head back to 231 ●

●●●●

Frankenwrestler tosses the slab in your direction, and you jump up and perform a spin-kick, hoping to shatter it with your foot. Instead, though, the slab shatters YOU. It was a nice try, but this match is already over, and . . .

YOU ARE DEAD. CONTINUE: Y/N?
Y: Head to 48 ● N: Head to 265 ●●●●

●

You're running forward and decide to try to go OVER your problem instead of through it by jumping into the air—no, jumping into the sea. You hear the muffled *SPROING* and at first your leap looks like it's about to take you clear over the Noctopus, but instead you seem to be falling short, directly down toward the head of the beast. It looks bleak, but you land solidly on the Noctopus's head near its eyebrows with your heavy boots. The creature recoils in pain and retreats into the darkness of the Serendipity Sea. Nice!

Head to 16 ●

●●

You forgo grabbing a torch, figuring that the time you spend trying to free one from the wall is better spent running from spiders. Continuing up the seemingly endless stairs, you can barely stay ahead of your gruesome pursuers. You're beginning to get tired, and even though you're the Champ, you feel yourself slowing down. They're getting closer . . . closer . . . closer . . . closer, until suddenly you are tackled from behind by a gang of spiders! They crawl all over you, rapidly spinning a web that encases you before you can scream for help. This looks like the end, Champ. We hate to say it, but . . .

YOU ARE DEAD. CONTINUE: Y/N?
Y: Head to 62 ● **N: Head to 265** ●●●●

●●●

You shoot your speargun and watch as a bolt disappears harmlessly into the darkness. That was a whole lot of nothing. Choose another action quickly, though—your air gauge beeps again, and it's warning you that you're almost out of oxygen.

Head back to 16 ●

It doesn't make any sense, but you pull your wheel to the left and head directly toward the narrow opening in the side of the mountain. The pothole is coming up, but you make it into the tunnel just before you fall into the chasm! But now you're in the dark. Dim lights illuminate your way somewhat, but one false move and you'll probably end up smeared against the close walls on either side of you.

Ahead of you there is something shiny in the middle of the road, a glittering object that you hope isn't going to damage your car, because there's no way around it. You rapidly get closer to it, and you see that it's actually a silver coin bouncing up and down. Its bounce times perfectly with your approach, and you grab it in midair as you pass. Awesome catch!

CONGRATULATIONS!
YOU FOUND . . .

ONE OF THE
SILVER COINS!

Moments later a light appears at the end of the tunnel—it's an exit! You pass through and find yourself back on the track, the Ernesto puppet car nearby, its wooden driver staring at you with a wooden smile.

Head to 185 ●●●●

Your enemies routed, you sprint up the remaining stairs, torch in front of you to ward off any straggling spiders, and moments later, you reach the top of the staircase. Turning to face the way you came, you can see that some spiders have escaped the carnage and are still pursuing you! Well, you know how to deal with THEM—raising the torch to the cobwebs that line the stairwell, you set fire to them instantly, turning the corridor into an inferno. You smile as the remaining spiders sizzle, and then, dusting off the remaining cobwebs, you take stock of your surroundings: You're at another door, from behind which you hear the buzzing and crashing sounds of electrical machinery. Light spills out from beneath the door, flashing off and on intensely. Behind you is a stairwell that's the home of giant spiders. Ahead is the unknown. Having had your fill of massive arachnids, you decide that the only way to go is forward. Something invisible agrees with you, it seems, for the door opens on its own. Squinting into the bright light emanating from ahead, you enter!

Head to 48 ●

WRESTLEVANIA ROUND TWO

You find yourself in what looks to be a large, old-fashioned monster-making lab, the kind imagined in a book by Mary Shelley you once read, complete with a host of bizarre-looking equipment scattered here and there. You walk to the center of the room and look up: Above you, the roof is open, exposing the room to the elements, and you can see that the lightning storm is still raging outside. There's also some sort of platform

suspended up there, hanging from chains, but you can't see what's on it. The walls of the lab are lined with strange machinery with massive dials and bizarre displays that you can't understand. Electricity arcs between the poles of a Jacob's ladder, and the entire scene is one of chaos and madness. It's frightening but, you must admit, pretty cool.

It's then that you notice that you are not alone in the lab, for standing nearby at a device with a massive lever is someone dressed in a lab coat. The figure turns to face you, and you can see that the mad scientist is none other than DRACULA!

"Velcome, Champ! Velcome to my lab! It is here that I engage in one of my many hobbies—mad science!" The vampire laughs evilly. "You haff arrived just in time to fight your next match. Ha-ha-ha!"

At Dracula's words, electricity courses through four Tesla coil–style devices, which form a square around you, and four sections of chain-link fence rise out of the floor between each of the coils, forming an electrified prison around you! You're trapped!

"Yes, Champ! Your next match is a CAGE MATCH!"

With those words, lightning strikes the platform above you, filling it with energy, and Dracula flips a switch, causing the platform to descend toward the ring. "And here comes your next opponent! Beware—they might be . . . familiar to you!"

As the platform comes to a stop, you can see that something is lying on the slab, covered by a sheet. A moment passes, then another, and you watch the immobile form. Then . . . a movement! An arm rises, then another, and the figure sits up, and you see that the thing below the sheet is someone you know. SomeONES you know—it's Boris and Elsa, their scarred bodies fused into one grotesque two-headed wrestler! But how?

"I recovered the bodies of your friends and realized

that it vas the perfect opportunity to try out a little experiment I had in mind." Dracula laughs as his body transforms under his lab coat, shifting into the form of a bat. "I gave them life once again as the strangest tag team of them all! Meet . . . FRANKENWRESTLER!"

His transformation complete, Dracula flies out of the lab and into the stormy night sky, leaving you to face the creature that used to be your friend(s). Using its terrific strength, the Frankenwrestler lifts the slab it was resurrected upon over its heads.

"You belong . . . ," says Boris's head.

" . . . DEAD!" finishes Elsa's.

And with that, lightning strikes again, and Frankenwrestler makes to throw the slab . . . at you! The match has begun!

Boris and Elsa—Frankenwrestler—have thrown the slab they were reanimated on directly at you. You don't think that's a legal move, but hey, this is Transylvania. What's your next move?

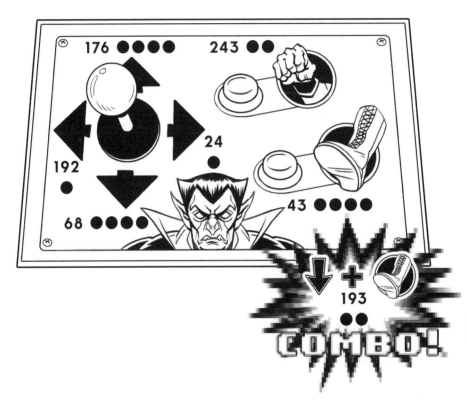

●●

You turn and walk away from the paintings and continue down the hall until they're behind you. You walk for a few minutes until you see something coming up ahead of you . . . the paintings! Somehow you've come back to exactly where you just were. Weird. But Dracula DID just challenge you to a match, so you're dealing with new levels of weirdness here. Do something else.

Head back to 66 ●●●

●●●

That way is blocked by a wall of thorny plants. You can't go in this direction. Aim yourself in some other direction.

Head back to 197 ●

●●●●

Hoping to skirt around the monster that seems intent on doing something nasty to you, you try to move to the right, but the spider seems to be able to read your thoughts and prevents you from going any farther. Do something else . . . quick!

Head back to 92 ●●●

You gaze at the tower ahead of you, but something tells you that you should try to exit the ring in the opposite direction. You move that way and squeeze through the rope vines, coming up against the thick brambles of the forest. Your way is blocked. But only for a moment, as the branches and roots of the trees mysteriously begin to pull back, revealing a SECRET PATH into the forest! Feeling compelled to see what is at the end of the footpath, you begin to walk . . .

Head to 109 ●●

●●

The bridge you're on is too narrow, and you can't go that way. You can only go forward. Quick—do something else before you end up a part of the gate!

Head back to 238 ●

●●●

You beat a hasty retreat into the fire behind you. That was NOT smart. Remember: Only YOU can prevent wrestler fires. Sadly . . .

YOU ARE DEAD. CONTINUE: Y/N?
Y: Head to 63 ●●● N: Head to 265 ●●●●

●●●●

You walk toward the lip of the lid . . . and promptly slip off the edge, falling down, down, down, down . . .

Down, down, down, down, down, down . . .

DOWN, down, down, down, down, down . . .

Wow. You really WERE a long ways up, weren't you?

. . . down, down, down, down, down . . .

Oh, heck. There's no way around it.

YOU ARE DEAD. CONTINUE: Y/N?

Y: Head to 242 ●●●● **N:** Head to 265 ●●●●

●

You try to push El Hombre Lobo over on his back, using your leverage, but his werewolf agility is too much to overcome. Try something else!

Head back to 14 ●●

●●

WHISH! You saw through the humid air of the Groovy Gardens sewer with the greatest of ease, but there's nothing there to cut in half, so that was pretty much useless. Try another tactic.

Head back to 231 ●

●●●

You and Dracula rush toward each other and meet in the middle of the ring, fingers interlaced, his strength against yours. Each of you struggles mightily to gain the upper hand, but neither of you can push the other one over. Finally, you break apart, panting from the effort and still at odds. Try another move!

Head back to 70 ●●●●

You blink your eyes once, then twice. You're groggy and shake your head, finally waking up after what feels like an eternity. Looking around, you see that you are no longer outside. Instead, you're inside a grand chamber, its walls made from stone, a great fire burning in a fireplace at the end of the room, before which is a large, throne-like chair, its back to you. Through the narrow windows of the chamber, you can see that the storm is still raging outside. You must be somewhere inside that castle you saw! But . . . how did you get here?

"If you are vondering how you came to be here," says a velvety yet cruel-sounding voice that seems to be emanating from behind the chair, "vonder no longer. It vas *I* who brought you here!"

A tall, black-haired man dressed in antique formal wear gets up from the chair and turns toward you with a flourish of the cape hanging on his shoulders. "I bid you velcome . . . CHAMP." He smiles at the look of surprised shock on your face.

"Yes, I know who you are, and I know vhere you vere going. You and your friends vere on a barnstorming tour of Europe, taking on all comers in no-holds-barred wrestling matches, but little did you know that the greatest wrestler around vas HERE, in TRANSYLVANIA! Yes, I, Count Dracula, should be the vearer of that belt!"

Wait a minute—Count Dracula is an AMATEUR WRESTLER?! You begin to laugh, but your moment of mirth is cut off as a deafening combination of lightning and thunder booms, and the man's face and form change instantly, going from handsome-but-sinister man to ugly-and-terrifying bat-monster—it's the same creature you saw on the plane! Moving with supernatural quickness, the creature rushes toward you and tries to pull your championship belt from around your waist, only to recoil when it touches it, its clawed hand smoking.

"Aaaarrrghh!" cries the vampire as it withdraws. "I see. The belt is protected by some sort of mystic protection that must be veakened before I can claim it. But make no mistake: The belt VILL be mine!"

The creature—Count Dracula—raises its gnarled, injured hand and points at you. "If you vish to escape my clutches, you must travel through my castle, survive my cunning traps, vanquish my fearsome minions, and defeat creatures of the night in monstrous wrestling matches, ultimately facing ME! If you succeed, you vill go free. But if I vin, I, Count Dracula, vill be the champion! Ha-ha-ha! And you vill be . . ."

You hear the sound of a bell being rung, like at the beginning of a wrestling match, as lightning erupts from the count's fingers, lightning bolts that twist into letters forming words that float in the air before you.

The lightning glows bright, so bright that it blinds you for a moment, and then fades to nothingness, leaving behind the smell of burnt something and an empty room. Your adversary has vanished! Looking around, you see that the room has only one open door, behind you. Through it is a hallway, from which echoes the sound of a wolf howling. You know that you must now find your way out.

So: What's your next move?

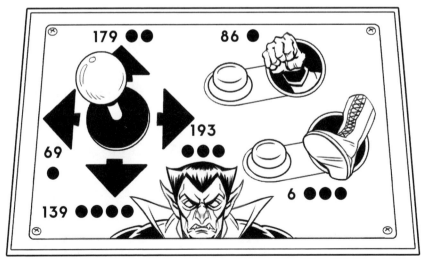

●

You hustle up the stairs, taking them two and three at a time now, hoping that you'll lose the spiders and get to your next wrestling opponent all the sooner. But as you move, you can't help but notice that numerous torches line the wall of the stairwell, lighting the way. An idea occurs to you: Maybe you should pause for a second and risk the spiders catching up to you to grab a torch? Or should you continue up the stairs?

If you think it's not worth the risk and continue running, head to 44 ●●

If you risk being caught by the spiders to grab a torch, head to 163 ●

●●

Mysteriously, you decide to run into the arms of the Noctopus. Why? How is that an option? Welp, the Noctopus eagerly reaches out with its tentacles and pulls you closer to its monstrous mouth. You almost reached the shore, but now . . .

YOU ARE DEAD. CONTINUE: Y/N?
Y: Head to 167 ●●● N: Head to 265 ●●●●

You hustle forward in the hallway, and you can see an open door mere feet ahead, beyond which looks to the outside . . . and freedom! You make a break for it, hoping that you can get past the next chandelier before it falls, but you're too late—it crashes to the ground in front of you, blocking your way. You have seconds before the flames ahead of you and the flames behind you make you into a toasted wrestler sandwich. What's your next move?

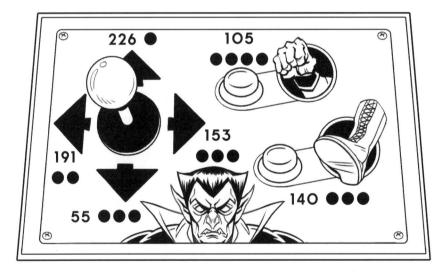

226 ●

105
●●●●

153
●●●

191
●●

140 ●●●

55 ●●●

●●●●

Dracula lies on the mat, befuddled by your tripping move. What's next? How are you going to wrap up this vampire jabroni and bury him for good?

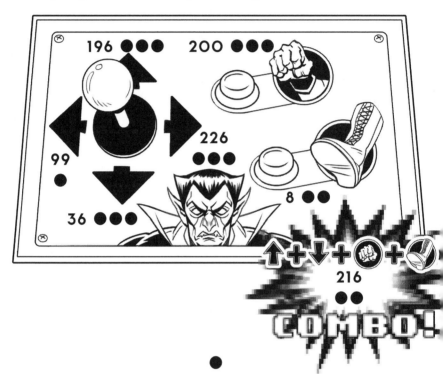

●

You stubbornly try to claw your way through the wall of branches and brambles to your left in the hopes of finding some sort of hidden passage through the Groovy Gardens, but all you get for your efforts are scratched hands. Choose again!

Head back to 228 ●●●

ERNESTO

The door to the
beach hut creaks open, and you creep
inside, slowly moving around the sparse
quarters. There's hardly any furniture in the

place besides an old sea chest and a table and chair, and the only decorations are old faded posters of the original Excellent Ernesto Cousins. This place wasn't used for much, apparently. It was probably just a spot to get out of the sun for a bit or . . . to change clothes! That's it! A change of clothes! The *Excellent Ernesto Cousins* games always involved a new outfit somewhere along the way. Maybe the sea chest is storing exactly that. Interesting. You stand before the large container. Do you open it?

If Y, head to 95 ●●●

If N, head back to 201 ●●●●

●●●

You travel farther down the hallway, hoping to find the source of the breeze and escape, and you come upon something decidedly strange: a small gallery of paintings. There are three of them in a row, and the cracks in the paint and dust on their frames make them look as if they were painted a very long time ago. But . . . they appear to be depicting climactic moments of WRESTLING MATCHES. Modern wrestling matches, but done in a gloomy, Gothic style as befits your surroundings.

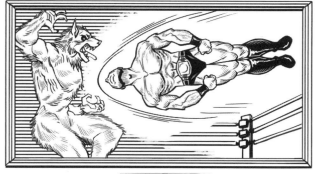

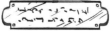

Beneath each painting is a small brass plaque, the words on each obscured by years of grime and dust. You are facing the paintings. What's your next move?

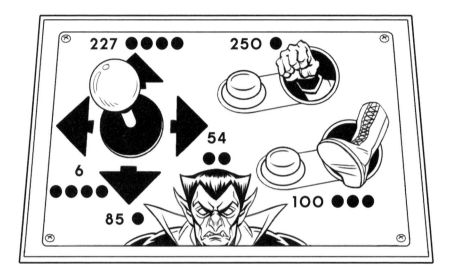

You hustle backward to buy some time, but you get a nasty surprise when your back touches the "ropes" and an electric shock courses through your body. That way isn't going to work. You've gotta avoid the borders of the ring. Choose another move!

Head back to 48 ●

●

You move to the side of the chamber, but there's nothing here but musty heads of stuffed animals, hunting trophies from long ago. Ick. Go somewhere else.

Head back to 58 ●●●●

●●

Sproing! You jump up and grab on to the ladder, uncontrollably reaching hand over hand, and suddenly you're climbing all the way back up to the surface.

Head to 41 ●

●●●

You juke to the right, and Dracula is there before you know it, almost as if he's using his vampiric mind-reading powers to anticipate your move. For a moment you consider alerting the hunchback to your suspicions, but you realize that in this situation, YOU'RE the heel, not Dracula. Who cares if he's cheating? Try again.

Head back to 70 ●●●●

●●●●

You finally reach the ring, which this time actually has nothing supernatural or weird about it—it seems like a regulation ring, the kind you're used to wrestling in; but as you slip through the ropes, you remind yourself that NOTHING is what it seems here in Dracula's domain. The crowd is still roaring, hissing, and jeering at you as you walk around the ring. Let 'em yell! You. Are. The. Champ!

As you taunt the crowd, the hunchback raises his arms to placate the crowd and begins to speak into the microphone again. "That's right, that's right! Give the challenger a warm Wrestlevania welcome! Yeahhhhhh!" More trash rains down upon you. "But enough of that. You're here to see your hometown hero. You call him your Dark Lord, but I call him Master . . . of Disaster! Please welcome . . . DRACULA!"

A thundering heavy-metal version of "Swan Lake" begins as the lights dim and a spotlight catches a fluttering object descending from the ceiling. Whatever it is, the crowd goes WILD when they see it, and even wilder when it begins to circle down toward the ring. It's not just any object—it's a MONSTROUS BAT, and it's flying straight toward YOU! As it passes over your head, you duck to avoid it, and it whirls around the ring before

it twists and transforms into its true form—DRACULA! When they see him, the crowd screams. You certainly have your work cut out for you.

The king of the *nosferatu* has learned a thing or two about working a crowd, because every time he bares his fangs at them and raises his cape theatrically, the assembled fiends eat his act up. Then he snatches the microphone from the hunchback, who scurries out of the ring and takes a spot at a bell that hangs nearby. Holding the microphone to his mouth, Dracula points at you.

"I vant you all to bid velcome to this evenink's challenger, the Champ!"

"BOOOOOOOOOOO!"

"So RUDE! Ha-ha-ha-ha-ha-ha! So, are you ready to see a REAL Monster Mash? Give it up if you are!"

The crowd howls with ghoulish glee, and Dracula smiles with smug satisfaction. He holds a hand up, and the crowd quiets down.

"But you didn't rise from the grave to hear me talk, did you? No? You vant action, you get action!" The microphone rises back up, into the darkness, and Dracula grabs his shirt with both hands and RIPS OFF his formal vampire suit, revealing wrestling trunks and boots underneath—he came prepared! Then his face contorts, changing into a fierce mask of vampire teeth and bat-like features as his body bulks up into a mass of rippling muscles.

"This is a no-holds-barred match, Champ," Dracula says. "No rules. Only a vinner and a loser. Are you ready? Dracula is ready!"

The hunchback rings his bell eagerly. The match has begun!

Dracula stands before you, a stack of vampire muscle ready to throw down. He snarls at you, and his eyes glow red with fury. He wants this victory. Do you want it more? Then you'd better play for your life!

Nope. Going that way isn't going to help. That's a wall. The only way out is ahead. Think fast and choose again.

Head back to 20 ●●

●●

You rush toward the wrasslin' werewolf, hoping to take him down with a swift elbow or a clothesline, but he dodges your attack with preternatural werewolf speed and CHOMPS DOWN on your arm, grasping it tightly and pulling you to the mat. You can't pull free no matter what you do. El Hombre Lobo raises his head and releases an epic howl at the moon before turning his attention back to you, drool dripping from his jaws. Not only are you pinned . . .

YOU ARE DEAD. CONTINUE: Y/N?
Y: Head to 171 ●●● N: Head to 265 ●●●●

●●●

Thinking you can sprint along the railing and make your way around the boarded-up section of the pathway, you jump up onto the wood . . . which immediately breaks under your weight. You land on nothing, missing the floating path entirely on your way down and speedily descending into the mist below, which technically means you DIDN'T land. Not YET, that is . . .

YOU ARE DEAD. CONTINUE: Y/N?
Y: Head to 119 ●● N: Head to 265 ●●●●

••••

Something about the *Excellent Ernesto Cousins 3* cabinet compels you to come closer, and as you do, you note that the game has a subtitle—the full name of the game is *Excellent Ernesto Cousins 3: Third Cousins.* You also note that while the imagery on the machine retains the bright primary colors and cartoony style of the famous *Excellent Ernesto Cousins* games you're familiar with, the art itself has a decidedly . . . gloomy bent to it, as if the entire cast of the game got trapped in a postapocalyptic wasteland of some sort. It's a weird juxtaposition, but you chalk that up to the flight of fancy of some overimaginative artist unfamiliar with the gee-whiz, aw-shucks vibe of the exploits of Ernesto and his cousin Miguel, two enterprising carpenters who embark on wild, lighthearted adventures in the mystical Dandelion Kingdom. As you get close to the machine, you can hear the chiming tones of the *Excellent Ernesto Cousins* theme song, its catchy melody bringing a warm smile of recognition to your face. *This is going to be fun,* you think as you quickly drop your Midnight Arcade token into the coin slot.

But everything changes the instant the strange coin reaches the depths of the machine and clunks into place; the music stops for a moment, as if there is a digital glitch somewhere inside the game, but it starts again almost instantly. It's the same tune, but now it's a little bit . . . eerie, as if the song itself were melting. You grab the game's joystick, and when you do, the Midnight Arcade shakes once, violently. You look over to the arcade's attendant—he grins and shrugs. Shaking your head, you press the game's Start button.

And that's when EVERYTHING begins to shake, every machine around you, all the dusty lights above you; everything is vibrating wildly. The other arcade cabinets start to scoot across the floor, looking as if they're about to fall over. It's an earthquake! You try to let the joystick go so you can flee, but something is keeping your hand attached. The game's GOT YOU! And that's when you notice that the ground around you appears to be splitting apart. There are small cracks at first, but those cracks quickly turn into large cracks, and in short order the ground opens up into wide chasms that begin to swallow machines whole. Then, one of those chasms opens underneath your feet, and you and the *Excellent Ernesto Cousins* machine fall into the new hole, which seems to have no bottom. As you plummet down into nothingness, you can't help but notice that you're no longer attached to the joystick, and that you're falling farther and farther away from the heavy box. That's good, right?

And then . . . *oof*! Your breath is forced out of your lungs as your fall has been suddenly arrested by something—the ground! *Where did THAT come from?* you wonder. Just a second ago, you were in a void, and now you're on the dusty earth. Standing up, you brush the dirt off your clothes, which have somehow changed into a worker's outfit, complete with a saw hanging from a loop in the tool belt fastened around your waist. Weird.

Looking around, you realize that you're at the crossroads of what appears to be some sort of village that has seen better days—curvy and rounded houses that look like they were once brightly painted are now run-down shacks, boarded up and abandoned. Junk and trash has accumulated at three sides of the town center, and the only open pathway before you is pitted with potholes, leading to a bleak horizon. But there are also floating platforms ahead of you, weird terraces somehow hovering in the air. But . . . how?

That's when it hits you, and you realize where you are: You're in DANDELION VILLAGE, the home of the Dandies, the cute average citizens of the Dandelion Kingdom and the bucolic hub of activity in the *Excellent Ernesto Cousins* games. But what happened? Why is it so messed up? And where are all the Dandies?

And that's when you see them, emerging from behind hanging doors, peeking their heads through the gaps in the boarded-up windows—it's the Dandies, but they look just as worn-out as their village, dressed in rags and roughly sewn together clothes, glancing around fearfully, as if they're HIDING from something. But what?

Soon, you're surrounded by a crowd of the pathetic creatures, who reach out to you in wonder, like they've been waiting for you for a long time and they can't

believe you've finally arrived. The control panel of the *Excellent Ernesto Cousins 3* arcade cabinet flashes on and off in your vision, and you know that you need to make some sort of move.

What do you think you should do?

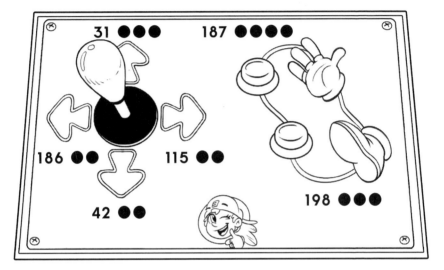

You decide to explore whatever is under the Groovy Gardens, and grasping the sides of the ladder, you carefully descend into the large drainage pipe. The steps on the ladder are slick with slime and damp water, and a couple of times on the way down, your feet slip and you nearly lose your grip and fall. But you manage to hang on and make it all the way down, finally reaching the bottom of the ladder, which ends at the beginning of what looks to be a sewer pipe large enough to walk in. Behind you is a wall where the sewer dead-ends. You hear the sound of water flowing. Reaching down, you pull out the flashlight conveniently hanging on the lower rungs of the ladder and shine it into the distance. Do you want to continue, or do you want to climb back up the ladder?

If you want to continue down the underground pipe, head to 231 ●

If you want to climb back up the ladder, head back to 41 ●

●●

As Dracula rushes your way, you move to the right and let him pass by harmlessly. He's really angry now, and he comes back around for another go! Choose another move.

Head back to 169 ●●●●

●●●

Tentacles shoot and slink toward you with alarming speed, but you roll to the right and deftly dodge them. That's not going to keep the creature at bay for long, though—pick another move!

Head back to 39 ●

●●●●

The chandelier falls, and as it does, you attempt to grapple with it as if it were a flaming foe! You feel the weight of the enormous piece of ancient decorative lighting push you toward the ground, intent on crushing you. But you've timed it just right, and you feel a reservoir of strength well up within you—and you toss your burden behind you, smashing it into pieces!

Head to 63 ●●●

You rush to take one of the remaining seats as turbulence rocks the plane from side to side. You turn to look out the window: Yep, the wing's still on fire. That's not all that's out there, though, and you have to blink to make sure you're not seeing things; but even after you rub your eyes, you can still see it—sitting on the wing is a MAN dressed in old-fashioned evening wear. But it's not a man, not really. It's something *shaped* like a man, but with large, leathery WINGS under its arms. And then it looks at you, and you find yourself faced with the eyes of something that's half human, half bat! What IS that thing? It hisses at you and then jumps off the wing, flying off into the storm as another bolt of lightning strikes the wing, severing it from the fuselage and sending the plane into a spin.

"Mayday, Mayday!" says the pilot over the radio. "Hold on, wrestlers—we're going down!"

And the last thing you think in the seconds before your plane strikes the side of a nearby mountain is, *Dang, we should've jumped*. You've barely started playing *Wrestlevania* and already . . .

YOU ARE DEAD. CONTINUE: Y/N?

Y: Head to 126 ●●●● **N: Head to 265** ●●●●

● ●

You scuttle backward, away from the mad dash of Frankenwrestler, and back directly into the electrified ropes of the ring! You recoil from the electric current that courses through your body and try to pull away, but in an instant you are wrapped up in the arms of your opponent and pinned against the barrier! It's using the ropes, and it doesn't seem to care that the electricity is cooking BOTH of you! What a way to win—and LOSE!

YOU ARE DEAD. CONTINUE: Y/N?
Y: Head to 33 **● ●** **N:** Head to 265 **● ● ● ●**

● ● ●

You walk directly into the crab creature's pinching claws, which are not-so-surprisingly VERY strong, given its size and general bad disposition. It's those claws that grab you and will not let you go, no matter how much you thrash and struggle. This is it. You've met your end in a grubby surfer's shack in a down-at-the-heels fantasy world. Guess what?

YOU ARE DEAD. CONTINUE: Y/N?
Y: Head to 12 **● ● ●** **N:** Head to 265 **● ● ● ●**

●●●●

Maybe there's a secret way this way? Nope. There isn't. There are only vines, leaves, dust, and spiky plant-thingies that poke holes in your digital skin. Pick another action.

Head back to 228 ●●●

●

You back up to get a better look at the paintings. From your new perspective, you admire them even more. Whoever the artist was, they had some skill, and you wish you could take these works home and hang them in your boring beach bedroom. But you can't, so try something else.

Head back to 66 ●●●

●●

You can't go that way! You've got no time to spare, and moving backward won't help. Choose another action.

Head back to 16 ●

● ● ●

You move to the left, circling El Hombre Lobo and being careful to stay out of the creature's reach, but as you do, your transformed friend gets to his knees, then to his paws, and then howls a challenge to you—you should have attacked when you had the chance! It's back to the beginning of the match!

Head back to page 171 ● ● ●

● ● ● ●

You steer to the right, and the buzz saw zips by on your left, passing so close that it leaves a scar in the side of your car and you can smell the scent of freshly sawed wood. You see dust—no, you saw dust. Still, it missed! Your celebration is short-lived, though, for your pursuer shoots at you again. Choose another move!

Head back to 7 ●

●

You reach out and grab the nearest piece of furniture, a chair, hold it over your head, and then throw it toward the fire, where it shatters into kindling and then burns. Hmm. Interesting, but not helpful. Pick another move.

Head back to 58 ● ● ● ●

• •

You hustle forward, and the mist curls around your ankles as you do, pulled along in your wake, and rapidly fills in the space behind you, seemingly walling off your way back. It makes sense, you figure, recalling that in the original *Excellent Ernesto Cousins* game, once you moved forward, you couldn't retrace your steps. There was literally no going back, and it seems that this level of the game is a throwback to that vintage design. Okay, cool. Got it. This level goes one way and one way only.

Soon, however, you feel like you're retracing your steps and notice that things are starting to look familiar— you've somehow come back to where you started, once again staring down the long hallway of green, standing above the stone with the odd epigram. You've been warped back to your original position! Time to choose another direction.

Head back to 228 • • •

• • •

You move to your left, toward the vine ropes of the ring. Beyond is the intractable haunted forest, impassable. You can't go this way.

Head back to 25 • •

You brake your car to a complete stop after rolling through the gate, and once the sawdust cloud dies down, you see that you're in the middle of Ernestopia, or, rather, what SHOULD be Ernestopia. What looked like a grand village from the outside is, on the inside, nothing more than false fronts of buildings, held up by large wooden beams. Ernestopia is FAKE. There's nothing here. Nobody. Your travels through the Groovy Gardens, under the Serendipity Sea, and over the road to Ernestopia have been for, literally, nothing. You kick the floor, frustrated. What the heck? This is decidedly NOT Excellent.

But wait—there actually is something in this empty shell of a city. Against the far wall there are two enormous wooden statues, replicas of the Excellent Ernesto Cousins, standing stock-still and looking out over the horizon. And even closer, sitting in the middle of the vast clearing that should be the city, is a tall wooden box with glass windows set in each side. You lightly step on the gas and drive your car over to the weird object, and as you get close to it, you see that inside it is actually an intricate wooden carving of the famous Ernesto of the Excellent Ernesto Cousins from the waist up. Upon further inspection, you notice that it's finely articulated

down to the smallest detail, and that its wooden eyelids are shuttered closed. A sign above the carving advertises the machine (for this is certainly a wooden machine, like your car) as "Excellent Ernesto Explains." It's just like one of those old fortune-telling machines that used to be in arcades, but it doesn't seem to be working, or at least not yet. You bang on the glass with your fist once. Twice. Then three times, and at that the automaton inside the machine blinks its wooden eyes open and smiles, revealing a stunning set of wooden dentures.

"'Tis I, Ernesto," it says, echoing its namesake's favorite catchphrase. "I'm so glad you made it all the way to the end of my little obstacle course. If you have any questions about the whys, the whats, and the wherefores of what just happened, I'm the wooden automaton to answer them.

"So: Do you have something for me?" the wooden Ernesto says. "Do you have any of my silver coins? I set them about the Dandelion Kingdom in the hopes that someday someone would come along and best the challenges I set before them, and I sense that you might have accomplished that. The more coins you found, the more I will tell you about what happened here. Insert your coins now." Looking down, you can see that the machine has a flat coin slot with slots for three coins, the type of mechanism that you lay the coins in and then push the plunger. It's an old-time arcade machine inside a retro arcade game. Weird!

If you found no coins, head to 230 ●●●●

If you found one coin, head to 3 ●●●

If you found two coins, head to 189 ●●●●

If you found three coins, head to 234 ●●●●

●

Seeing that El Hombre Lobo is incapacitated, you lean down and strike the beast, and he recoils from the force of your blow, rolling over on the mat but staying down. Choose another move!

Head back to 199 ●

●●

You stay in your lane, hoping that the buzz saw won't catch up with you, but the sound of the saw cutting through your car's rear end means that it did much, MUCH more than catch up. You were SO close, but . . .

YOU ARE DEAD. CONTINUE: Y/N?

Y: Head to 7 ● N: Head to 265 ●●●●

●●●

You begin your ascent up the wide stairs, which twist to your left, seemingly endlessly. But your wrestling-trained calves don't mind the exercise, and you go ever upward, toward what you figure will be another supernatural grapple. As you walk, you psych yourself up for whatever's coming, brushing cobwebs away from your face. At first, the webs are sparse, the kind of thing you'd expect to be hanging in the dark corners of a vampire's castle, but the higher you go, the bigger and more complex the cobwebs become. *Gee whiz*, you think as you spit out some webs. *There sure are a lot of spiders in this castle. Dracula needs to call an exterminator.*

And that's when you hear it—a strange noise that seems to be coming from above you. The sound is weird and creepy, like a dozen legs running over a pile of dead leaves. Looking up, you realize that you were a little off count with the dozen legs. There are only eight of them, but eight legs are more than enough when they're attached to a spider the size of a dog climbing across the ceiling and looking down on you with numerous hungry eyes! Your shock at seeing this monstrosity lasts only a moment, for a second later the spider drops to the ground and skitters toward you.

Aaaaaaaaah! Act now!

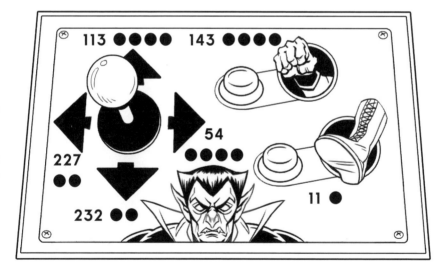

●●●●

You back away, awed by the fearsome Noctopus, but that moment of terror and reflection costs you immediately—you've run out of air! Turns out, the Noctopus didn't need to get you—you got yourself, and . . .

YOU ARE DEAD. CONTINUE: Y/N?
Y: Head to 167 ●●● N: Head to 265 ●●●●

●

You rush toward Frankenwrestler to meet its charge head-on . . . and it grabs you in its massive arms! You struggle to get free, but its science-enhanced arms are JUST. TOO. STRONG! It squeezes you tighter . . . tighter . . . tighter! And the last thing you hear before you black out is the ringing of the bell. You have lost the match . . . and your life!

YOU ARE DEAD. CONTINUE: Y/N?
Y: Head to 33 ●● N: Head to 265 ●●●●

●●

You pull back from El Hombre Lobo, taking the beast by surprise and pulling him off balance! Taking advantage of this opportunity, you plant your foot in his chest and flip him head over heels in a supernatural suplex, causing both of you to crash to the mat! But you're not as affected as El Hombre Lobo, and you get up while he lies there discombobulated.

Head to 199 ●

●●●

You reach down and flip up the latch on the unlocked sea chest. *Clunk!* Cautiously, you grab either side of the lid. You pause for a moment before throwing it open and simultaneously jumping back. A moment passes . . .

. . . and then a crab-like creature crawls from inside the chest.

Head to 12 ●●●

●●●●

As the Dandies continue their celebration, an older member of their tribe disengages from the rest and approaches you. This Dandy is grizzled almost to the point where he could be none-more-grizzled: He's stooped and walks with a cane, wears a cloak, and has a tattered patch over his right eye. If you didn't know any better, you'd say that this was a Dandy village elder of some sort, if not THE village elder.

"Greetings. I am the village elder," the old Dandy says. "I welcome you to our village. At last you have come, bearing the Mark, as was foretold years ago. Come to save the Dandelion Kingdom! Praise Ernesto!"

At this, the partying Dandies all echo the elder's words. "Praise Ernesto!" they chant. "Praise Ernesto!"

"The Mark?" you ask.

The Elder silently points to the saw on your tool belt and then to the patch sewn onto the left breast of your outfit. You look at it, and the understanding of how this game works begins to dawn on you.

"I was but a young Dandy when Ernesto and his cousin Miguel defeated Prince Dragon and his minions—for the second time—and saved the kingdom. They left us and our world to our own devices, trusting that we could govern ourselves. The cousins ate the Magic Mangoes, grew into giants, and strode their mighty long strides to the west, going beyond the Groovy Gardens, past the Serendipity Sea, and to the island of Ernestopia, where they retired to make great Bookshelves with their carpentry skills.

"For years we managed to rule ourselves, until *they* came, the monsters, laying waste to every level of the kingdom, until only our village remained. We hoped every night for the cousins to emerge and come to our aid. And now, you are here! A NEW carpenter, to write—or, rather, build—a bold new chapter in the saga of the Excellent Ernesto Cousins! You are the one we have been waiting for: You are the THIRD COUSIN!"

At this the Dandies cheer, giving the elder time to take a deep breath. That was a long speech for a rickety old fellow. "You must travel over land, under sea, and then beyond to find your cousins and bring them back to us. Go forth, brave carpenter, and save the Dandelion Kingdom!"

With these words, the crowd in front of you parts, clearing the way. Ahead of you is a path that leads out of the village and into what looks to be an enormous overgrown garden covered in a sinister mist. You understand that you really don't have a choice, and as a group of Dandelion Village musicians begins to play a folk version of the famously catchy *Excellent Ernesto Cousins* theme song, you draw your saw and run toward the garden. As you exit the village, you take note of a crude wooden sign on the side of the road:

There's no turning back now—your adventure has begun!

Head to 197 ●

●

Instead of going in for the kill, you warily circle Dracula to the left, and the ancient bloodsucker takes advantage of your hesitation, using the extra time to get to his feet. You had him, and you gave up the chance to pin him, and now he's ready to go again!

Head back to 70 ●●●●

SCREECH! You whip the car to the right, just barely avoiding the nest of nails in front of you. They could have really ruined your Sunday drive!

Head to 5

In the ultimate expression of art criticism, you leap at the paintings in an attempt to suplex them into revealing their deeper meaning, but a magical protective field blasts you back, stone-cold stunning you for a moment. Try something else (but please don't assault the art again).

Head back to 66

You hustle forward in the inimitable Excellent Ernesto Cousins fashion, deeper into the dark tunnels, your light bobbing up and down and illuminating . . . more tunnels. Endless tunnels. Tunnels, tunnels, tunnels. And then . . . a sound. Low at first, but as you walk farther on, you can make it out more clearly. It sounds like . . . a frog croaking? And a big one at that.

Head to 17

You exit the ring and begin to walk toward the castle, leaving El Hombre Lobo behind, trusting that he'll be safe lying unconscious in a haunted forest. Soon, you come to the walls of the castle and see that the fire is still raging inside the passageway you exited previously. You won't be able to get access to the tower here, so you start to walk along the perimeter of the castle, looking for some other access point. As you do, the electrical storm continues to rage above you, the lightning intermittently striking the towers above. You come to another entrance to the castle, an archway that leads to what looks like a spiral staircase winding upward toward the electricity-crowned tower. Feeling that this is the only way to go, you enter and begin to climb the stairs.

Head to 92 ●●●

Still armed with the speargun, you bring it up to your shoulder, holding it steady while you aim and the Noctopus gets closer . . . closer . . . and you shoot! The speargun's bolt scores a direct hit in the Noctopus's remaining eye, causing the monster to scream in pain and its tentacles to flail about wildly as it slinks backward into the Serendipity Sea. You slowly crawl backward up the beach until you're sure the Noctopus has had enough and isn't going to come back AGAIN, and then you stand and remove the diving suit and throw your speargun to the side. *Enough of that stuff*, you think as you grasp your saw. It's time to go back to the classics. And with that, you turn your back to the water and head up the beach, determined to reach the end of this wild game.

Head to 182 ● ● ●

● ● ●

You reel back, recoiling from the onslaught of terrifying trash, and as you do, you slip on a puddle of spilled blood soda, landing on your back. Unfortunately, the crowd takes advantage of your misstep and, fueled by their bloodlust, the assembled ghouls, ghosts, and vampires descend upon you. You've forfeited the match . . . by dying!

YOU ARE DEAD. CONTINUE: Y/N?
Y: Head to 154 ●● N: Head to 265 ●●●●

●●●●

The walls of the passageway certainly are something, aren't they? Stone and mortar. Yup—castle walls. Solid stuff. You can't walk through them, though, so try a different move.

Head back to 141 ●●●●

●

You press down on the brake pedal, and the car slows down. When you release the pedal, the car gets back up to speed. Test out the other controls or . . .

To test out the other controls,
head back to 182 ●●●

To continue on, head to 150 ●●

The crab creature is on its back, claws snapping wildly, its body rocking back and forth. It is clearly attempting to right itself and attack again. Think fast, cousin!

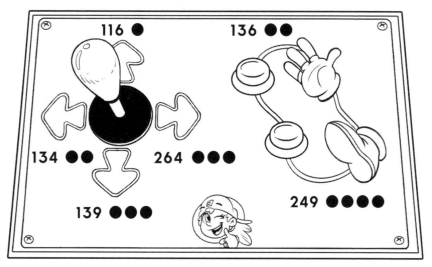

116 ●

136 ●●

134 ●●

264 ●●●

139 ●●●

249 ●●●●

●●●

You consider a dropkick, as it worked so well before with other animal monsters, namely the giant spiders. It's such an easy move that Dracula is actually caught off guard, and you knock him square in the fangs, sending him howling.

Head to 34 ●●●●

●●●●

You grab a handful of flaming-hot chandelier wreckage, and that goes just about as well as you might think it would. Hot hands equal lost life.

YOU ARE DEAD. CONTINUE: Y/N?
Y: Head to 63 ●●● **N:** Head to 265 ●●●●

Having stuck the landing, you turn to see the surface you were just standing on swallowed by the mist. This, you understand, means that there's no going back. Forward is where you're meant to travel, and that's where you're going to go. You look around and see that the strange skyway you're on, like the rest of the Dandelion Kingdom, is in a state of advanced disrepair. What once was probably a pretty nice promenade in the air is now a decidedly dangerous-looking gangplank, its wooden slats rotting, its railing rickety and in places nonexistent. You grab one of the waist-high railings and it crumbles, its parts falling down into the mist with you almost following, but you keep your balance and keep your grasp of the now-rotted railing piece. Shaking your head, you glance at the piece of wood in your hand and see that there's a small metal plaque.

BUILT BY THE
EXCELLENT
ERNESTO COUSINS
WITH PRIDE!

That's weird. In the story of the *Excellent Ernesto Cousins* games, the guys are carpenters who take pride in their work. But this stuff has become hazardous with neglect. What happened to the Dandelion Kingdom? Shrugging, you begin to walk forward down the path, carefully avoiding the holes that lead to nothingness and trying not to grab the railings when you feel a little uncertain. If there was a way up here, there has to be a way down, and you're going to find it.

And that's when you hear it: a sound coming from behind you, back in the clouds and mist. At first it sounds like the distant chugging of a . . . train? Up here in the sky? That's absurd! But you catch yourself—this whole PLACE is absurd. You can't see anything . . . until the mist parts, revealing that headed your way is nothing less than what looks like a living, breathing STORM CLOUD! A tornado beneath it propels it forward, rain falls from what seems to be its mouth, and lightning bolts crackle from its eyes. It's a Stormy, one of the enemies from the old *Excellent Ernesto* games! They used to look CUTE, though, and this one looks angry, much angrier than they ever looked in the past, and it's coming straight at you! Knowing that you can't fight the weather, you turn and begin to RUN away as fast as your feet can carry you!

You barrel forward along the pathway in the sky, a living storm cloud in hot pursuit behind you. Ahead of you, you see that there's a long gap in the path where a section of the promenade has fallen completely apart. You're running as fast as you can. What's your next move?

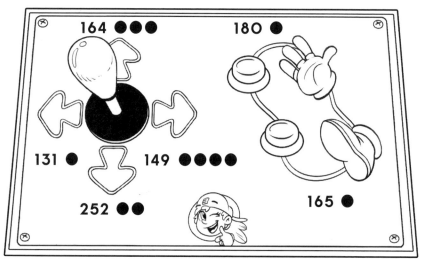

164 ●●●

180 ●

131 ●

149 ●●●●

252 ●●

165 ●

Soon, the twisting path in the woods leads you to another small clearing, but instead of a wrestling ring, there is a small hut there, a roughly constructed shanty big enough for one person. It's a studio hut! On its roof there is an old-fashioned TV antenna, and a glow emanates from its windows. What sort of creature calls this strange structure home? And why do you have the eerie sense that you've been here before?

The door opens and light spills out into the clearing, silhouetting a figure standing on the threshold shining a flashlight into the gloom of night.

"Who goes there?" asks the rough voice that comes from the figure. "I can hear ya sneakin' around out there. What are ya? Vampire? Werewolf? Ghoul? Whatever you are, g'wan. Git! Leave me to watch my TV in peace. I'm the ol' WWH—the Wrestling Watching Hermit—and I don't like company! You over there, at the edge of the wood! I see ya! Show yourself!"

Found out, you creep cautiously from your hiding place, hands up to show that you mean no harm. The figure edges forward and raises the beam of light, illuminating your face. You squint in the glare but aren't prepared for what happens next: The mysterious figure lets out a whoop of surprise and runs toward you excitedly.

"I can't believe it!" he says, and you see that your interrogator is a potbellied older gentleman with a mustache, wearing a trucker hat and a denim vest adorned with patches. "It's really you. THE CHAMP! Here, in my hermit's clearing in Transylvania. Come in! Come in and sit by the glow of my Selectra-Vision Colormatic!"

You follow the hermit inside his hut, which is roughly the size of an efficiency apartment. Wrestling memorabilia from around the world covers the walls. You scan the room and see a mini-fridge, a hot plate, and a sink stacked with dishes, and a couple of easy chairs in front of an antique-looking color television, upon which is displayed . . . a wrestling match! The Wrestling Watching Hermit offers you a seat, which you take, and puts a folding tray in front of you. Shuffling over to his toaster oven, he puts on oven mitts and withdraws a pair of TV dinners. "Something told me I was going to have company tonight," he says as he places a sectioned tray of once-frozen, now piping-hot food in front of you. You can't tell what any of it is, and it smells kind of weird, but you've been raised to be polite, so you say thank you, anyway. "I can't believe you're here, in my studio hut in Dracula's haunted forest. That's WILD. What are you even doing here?!"

You give the Wrestling Watching Hermit the lowdown on your situation around mouthfuls of weird food, starting with your plane going down, then Dracula's challenge, and ending with your match against El Hombre Lobo. He listens in fascination, and when you finish your story and your meal, he nods as he clears the dishes.

"You know, I've been watching all this happen on my TV, but I thought it was just a repeat of a match I'd never seen before," he says as he throws away your plastic tray, gesturing to his television. "Turns out the monstrous match of the century was LIVE. How 'bout that?" Seeing the look of confusion on your face, the hermit continues. "Yeah, this Selectra-Vision Colormatic is, like, magic or something.

"In fact, why don't you get closer and check it out?" he says, eyes widening. "The picture quality is really something else. The reception in this forest is UNREAL."

If you decide to get closer to the Selectra-Vision Colormatic, head to 145 ●●●

If you decline and decide to go back through the forest, head to 246 ●●●

●●●

You pull hard to the left, and the buzz saw passes by harmlessly on your right. After you avoid it, you pull back over to the center lane, just in time for the car to shoot ANOTHER buzz saw at you. Pick again!

Head back to 7 ●

●●●●

You run directly toward the spider . . . and it leaps up at you, jumping on your chest and quickly biting you with its fangs! Before you can react, you can feel the poison spread through your body; as you fall down, the last thing you see before you lose consciousness is the spider on top of you, and you know that . . .

YOU ARE DEAD. CONTINUE: Y/N?
Y: Head to 92 ●●● N: Head to 265 ●●●●

●

For some reason, you think that firing your weapon at a time that requires evasive driving action is a good idea. Well, you can think what you want, but you're wrong, at least in this instance. Your buzz saw weapon shoots off ahead of you and falls into the pot-CANYON, and you quickly follow it, and . . .

YOU ARE DEAD. CONTINUE: Y/N?
Y: Head to 23 ●● N: Head to 265 ●●●●

●●

You begin to kick your legs furiously, trying to get a leg-lock on the air around you, but that obviously does NOT work, as the air cannot wrestle. Instead of attempting to pin the wind, why don't you be a little bit more proactive and choose another action?

Head back to 222 ●

●●●

You leap—*SPROING!*—and your legs propel you up and OVER the gap so you land solidly on the path. Success! You made it across!

Head to 106 ●

●●●●

You move back and away from El Hombre Lobo, but he stays where he is, teeth gnashing, hungry for a fight but not ready to engage you . . . not yet, at least! Choose another move.

Head back to 171 ●●●

●

You move forward to get a closer look and . . . *BAM!* The tentacle whips forward with lightning speed, wrapping around your legs with a viselike grip, yanking you off your feet and dragging you toward the water. Other tentacles, also presumably attached to the same body as the cute eyes, reach out and begin to grab the bodies of the creatures washed up on the beach. Whatever this thing is, it's HUNGRY, and you are on the menu. You dig your fingers into the wet sand, but it's no use, and soon you're UNDERWATER. Shortly thereafter . . .

YOU ARE DEAD. CONTINUE: Y/N?
Y: Head to 201 ●●●● **N: Head to 265** ●●●●

●●

You attempt to get through the Dandies this way, but they link their arms together and begin to sway back and forth, singing what sounds like some sort of celebratory song . . . about you! But you can go no farther. Choose again.

Head back to 75 ●●●●

●●●

You hold your current position, as do the other cars. The road curves up to the right in a high bank, offering you a spectacular view of the rest of the island for a moment, and then curves back down. Pick another move.

Head back to 5 ●●

●●●●

You leap into the air and spin-kick a phantom opponent. You've still got it, Champ, but you don't need it. Not right now at least. Pick another action!

Head back to 25 ●●

●

You creep closer to the crab creature and nudge its body with your foot, testing to see how easily it could regain control. That little push almost gives it the momentum to flip back over to come after you again!

Head back to 104 ●●

●●

Imagining that you're pressing the joystick forward, you bring your arms down to your sides and straighten out your body, accelerating toward your friends and the weird flying fiend that seems to be pursuing them! You get closer . . . closer . . . closer, until you're almost near them . . . and then the weird monster flies up to you . . . and pulls your rip cord! The wind catches the billowing parachute, and you decelerate rapidly, watching as your friends drift into the clouds of the raging storm and then disappear from view. Your respite is short-lived, though, as the storm overtakes you and begins to whip you around. Hoping that the violence of the wind and rain doesn't rip a hole in your chute, you hang on for dear life as you get nearer to the ground. As you float downward, you look into the distance and see something extraordinary as the clouds briefly part: There's a castle nearby! But almost as soon as you see it, the clouds obscure it again, and moments later you're finally touching the earth in what has to be the worst landing ever, *clonk*ing the side of your head on a rock and falling unconscious . . .

Head to 58 ●●●●

You circle to the left of the Frankenwrestler's body, for some reason deciding not to press your advantage. That proves to be a mistake, for moments later it rouses itself and stands up, ready once again to wrestle.

It takes a swing at you, and you manage to dodge. But not for long . . .

Head to 33 ●●

●●●●

You press the button for your weapon, and the buzz saw flies away from you, bouncing harmlessly on the road before rolling off to the side. You didn't think that would work, and you were right. Wait—you didn't think that would work, did you? Make a new move!

Head back to 185 ●●●●

●

You walk into one of the corridor's walls like the confused wrestler you are. Don't do that! Escape! Figure out a better move—quick!

Head back to 20 ●●

●●

You scramble back to your feet and continue running, the Stormy in hot pursuit. The hairs on the back of your neck stand up from the electricity in the air. If you don't get out of here quick, the Stormy is going to wrap you in its weathery embrace, and you know that the results will be shocking and fatal. The path seems to lead on and on and on. You jump over more gaps, keeping just ahead of the Stormy, but there seems to be no end . . . wait! There's something ahead of you blocking the path! Yes, someone—or someTHING—has placed boards across the path and nailed them to the railing on either side. On the planks, there's a sign that says "NO TRESPASSING," and you're headed RIGHT TOWARD IT.

What is your next move?

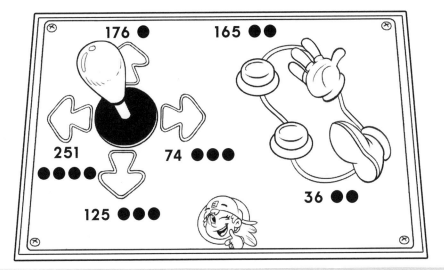

176 ●   165 ●●

251 ●●●●   74 ●●●

125 ●●●   36 ●●

You press the buzz saw button on your car's dashboard, which sends your edged projectile flying over the road. It passes above the nails—great!—and strikes the Ernesto puppet car that dropped them, cutting it in two—double great!—but you still drive over the nails, and the sharp tacks force your car into a hopeless spin that you can't recover from. You took one of them out, but they got the only one of you, so that means . . .

YOU ARE DEAD. CONTINUE: Y/N?
Y: Head to 150 ●● N: Head to 265 ●●●●

●●●●

Knowing a cue when you see it and realizing what the strange portrait in the hallway was telling you, you run toward El Hombre Lobo and leap into the air, coming down on the werewolf's body with both your leg AND your elbow. *BAM!* The ring shakes with the impact, and you quickly turn over, getting out of the creature's reach, but you don't think your precaution was necessary, for as you get up, you can see that your opponent isn't moving.

You've done it—you've delivered a perfect SILVER BULLET! YES!

Head to 25 ●●

●

The crowd on your right surges forward, and you move to the left . . . only to be caught in the clutches of the fiends on the left! You try to break free, but their bloodlust is just too strong, and they pull you into the crowd and fall on you, all fangs and claws and . . . Well, you get the idea. No more wrestling for you because . . .

YOU ARE DEAD. CONTINUE: Y/N?
Y: Head to 154 ●● N: Head to 265 ●●●●

●●

Speed has been the answer before, so maybe it'll be the answer now. At least that's your hope as you make your wooden car go faster, hoping that your momentum will shatter the gate to Ernestopia.

It was a decent plan, but . . . well, let's just say that you needed to be going a LOT faster than you were to break through that gate and spare you the terrible details of what happened next. All the same,

YOU ARE DEAD. CONTINUE: Y/N?
Y: Head to 238 ● N: Head to 265 ●●●●

●●●

You shuffle forward in your particular Ernesto Cousin style, hustling toward the water's edge. As you get closer, you notice a peculiar smell coming from the water. When you reach the shoreline, the smell is stronger and off-putting. Looking to your left and your right, you can see that the ocean has given up the bodies of more than a few of its denizens, and they're not doing so well in the sunshine. Yeesh. Probably best not to go any farther just yet, not until you're wearing something that will protect you in the water.

But as you retreat from the lapping of the ocean's waves, you notice something peering at you from the shallows—a pair of strange eyes are watching you, and they're . . . kind of cute, actually. You wave tentatively, and a tentacle (presumably attached to the eyes somewhere along the way) rises above the water and mimics your action. You move from side to side and the eyes (and now the tentacle) follow your every move, tracking you back and forth, like an interested pet.

Do you want to get a better look at this seemingly benign sea creature? What's your next move?

If you want get a closer look, head to 115 ●
If you want to choose another action,
head back to 201 ●●●●

●●●●

You continue to run forward and walk directly into the arms—no, tentacles—of the Noctopus. What a boneheaded move THAT was!

YOU ARE DEAD. CONTINUE: Y/N?
Y: Head to 132 ●●● N: Head to 265 ●●●●

●

You decide to investigate the beach shack, thinking that there might be something hidden inside that will guide you on your way or, at the very least, that it might contain some sort of treasure that will be useful to your progress. As you get closer, you see that the shack is in even worse shape than you thought initially—it looks dangerous and unsafe, like it would fall over in a light breeze and crush anybody inside.

Do you want to enter? Y/N?
If Y, head to 65 ●●
If N, head back to 201 ●●●●

The wind has picked up even more, and you're a little farther down the hallway, but there's still no sign of the exit. Looking up, you can see that another chandelier is about to fall. What's your next move?

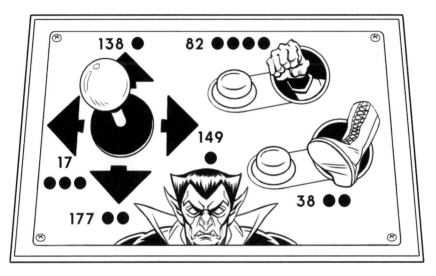

● ● ●

You pull back, slowing down before you reach the wall of boards across the path. You didn't run into the wall blocking your way—that's good!—but you did slow down enough for the Stormy to overtake you. There's no easy way to say this, so we'll come right out with it . . .

YOU ARE DEAD. CONTINUE: Y/N?
Y: Head to 119 ●● N: Head to 265 ●●●●

●●●●

You stand in front of the *Wrestlevania* machine, token in hand. The volume of its pounding theme tune—an electronic fusion of wailing '80s rock and Gothic classical music—has grown significantly since you approached it and is now practically blowing your hair back. You drop the token into the coin slot, place your hand on the joystick, and press the Start button.

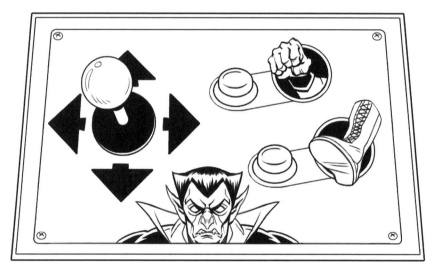

The moment you do, the music reaches a bombastic crescendo, and the fog begins to billow wildly, growing in volume until it envelops you fully and you can't even SEE the bright screen before you. And then an even stranger thing happens: You can hear the sound of a plane. Not in the distance, but all around you, as if you were ON one and not standing in a mysterious arcade. Letting go of the controls, you wave your hand in front of your face in the hopes of clearing away some of the fog, and it recedes, but you see immediately that somehow, you are no longer in the Midnight Arcade . . .

Instead, you're standing in the aisle of what appears to be a small airplane! It looks . . . antique, to say the least. It's not fancy at all, and a quick glance out the window reveals that you are flying at night through a raging thunderstorm. Lightning flashes outside, and the plane shudders in response, forcing you to brace yourself against the seats. Looking around, you see that you aren't alone. Sharing the small cabin with you are three other people: a man dressed in a snappy three-piece suit and a lucha libre mask and two hulking, glowering (and, let's be honest, quite ugly) bruisers dressed entirely in black. You've never seen these guys before, but you KNOW who they are: They're professional wrestlers! The man in the mask is El Hombre Lobo, a heroic idol of the ring, and the terror twins are Boris and Elsa, a tag team of heels. Feeling a heavy yet comfortable weight around your waist, you look down and see you're wearing a belt. A big belt. A CHAMPIONSHIP belt. They're wrestlers, and so are you! It's impossible, but there's no denying it:

Somehow you're INSIDE the game, inside *Wrestlevania*! And whatever's happening right now must be the introduction to the game. But what's about to happen?

BOOM! Another bolt of lightning cracks outside the plane, causing the engines to sputter and whine. Aha— THAT'S about to happen. *"Que lastima!"* says El Hombre Lobo, who closes his eyes, touches his head, chest, and shoulders with his fingers, and shakes his head. "Where did this storm come from so suddenly? One minute, the sky was clear. The next . . . *lluvia y relámpagos! Ay . . ."*

"Something weird's going on, Boris," says Elsa. "That's what we get for signing up for this crazy European barnstorming tour with a third-rate wrestling league."

"You said it, Elsa," agrees Boris. "I think it's the mountains we're flying over. They're HAUNTED."

As soon as Boris says that word, a chill runs down your spine, for you know that you're flying over the Carpathian Mountains, a range of peaks that is supposed to be the home of numerous monsters of legend. But that's all superstition. Monsters aren't REAL. Magic video game palaces are real, but monsters? Nah, that's RIDICULOUS.

KRAK-A-BANG! Another bolt of lightning arcs through the sky, this time striking the wing! The plane shakes violently, and you can now see that FLAMES are beginning to engulf the engine on that side. The plane is on FIRE!

The pilot turns around and yells, "You folks back there might have noticed that, uh, we've got a wing on fire, so brace yourselves and enjoy the ride while we try to find a spot to put this bird down. Or, if you're feeling lucky, uh, strap on a parachute and, well, jump."

You look at El Hombre Lobo. El Hombre Lobo looks at you and then at Boris and Elsa. Boris looks at El Hombre Lobo, Elsa looks at you, then the tag team looks at each other. Everybody's looking at everybody, and everybody is wide-eyed and scared.

What's your next move?!

If you decide to hope for the best, head to 83 ●

If you grab a parachute and jump out of the plane and into the storm, head to 222 ●

●

You move to the left, hoping that the Stormy won't react in time and will pass right by you . . . and it does! But your brilliant plan didn't take into account the fact that you'd have to lean up against one of the pathway's railings to make room for the Stormy to pass, and the rotted wood gives way thanks to your leaning. Arms wind-milling wildly, you stay upright and . . .

Aw, who are we kidding? This is a video game, not a cartoon. You fall and . . .

YOU ARE DEAD. CONTINUE: Y/N?
Y: Head to 106 ● N: Head to 265 ●●●●

●●

You leap toward El Hombre Lobo, but your plan of attack wasn't much of a plan at all. The creature grabs you in a werewolf version of a bear hug and begins to squeeze you without mercy!

YOU ARE DEAD. CONTINUE: Y/N?
Y: Head to 171 ●●● N: Head to 265 ●●●●

●●●

You hustle ahead, taking step after step in a funny, bounding way, hoping to find the surface before you run out of air. But there it is again—that feeling that something is nearby, checking you out, following you! You look behind and see nothing. Creepy. Then you turn your attention back to the path . . . and see that your way is blocked! A huge black cephalopod that looks like the creature on the sign rests in front of you, its long inky arms waving at you menacingly.

It's a NOCTOPUS! It's the thing that's been watching you, and now it looks like it's done watching and wants you for lunch. What's your next move?

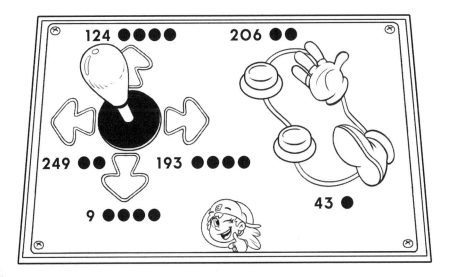

Realizing that the sooner you get to the ring the better, you rush through the rain of wretched garbage. You let it pelt you and keep your eye on your goal. The audience boos, but you reach the ring unscathed, if covered in gory fast food. That's the life of being a wrestler on the road!

Head to 70 ●●●●

●

You move to the left, thinking maybe you can sneak by the spiders by hugging the wall, but you've moved directly into the sticky cobwebs! You try to break free, but it's too late—you're trapped, and you can't swing the torch to defend yourself anymore. Sensing an opportunity, the spiders advance, cautiously at first and then quickly, all at once, crawling all over you in an instant. Guess what?

YOU ARE DEAD. CONTINUE: Y/N?
Y: Head to 163 ● **N: Head to 265** ●●●●

●●

You circle around the crab creature, looking for a weak spot, but you get a little too close during your inspection, and one of its flailing claws manages to hook into your Excellent Ernesto Cousin tool belt, pulling you toward its body and into its clawed embrace. Worst. Hug. EVER.

YOU ARE DEAD. CONTINUE: Y/N?
Y: Head to 104 ●● **N: Head to 265** ●●●●

●●●

Go faster? Why not! You only live once—or three times in a lot of games. You zoom toward the pothole, apparently hell-bent on crashing your car, but as you get closer you see that a portion of the road in front of you is actually bent, raised upward to become an accidental ramp. Your wheels leave the road, and your wooden roadster takes to the air, clearing the wide chasm ahead easily and then coming down in a jarring landing that shakes you but doesn't break you. You're still in this!

Head to 185 ●●●●

●●●●

You try to hold your car steady in your lane, but the Ernesto puppet car is too strong for you, and it pushes farther and farther to the left until you're grinding against the guardrail, quickly turning the side of your car into wood shavings. Try another move!

Head back to 185 ●●●●

●

Rushing toward Frankenwrestler, you decide to take advantage of the situation and deliver a flying elbow to your stunned opponent. *BAM!* The ring shakes from the impact, and you get up quickly and back away. Frankenwrestler groans in pain and doesn't get up! You're almost there, but try another move!

Head back to 258 ●●●●

●●

You figure that NOW is the perfect time to do crab carpentry, while your enemy is incapacitated, and while it isn't a claw cracker, you think your patented Excellent Ernesto saw is the right tool for the job. You bring it down in a chopping motion on the crab . . . and saw the sucker neatly in half! Wow, that's SHARP. Crab guts fly everywhere, including on you, but the crab creature is now crab dip. You beat it! Yuck, but hey: awesome, too!

Head to 220 ●●●

●●●

You move your body to the right and begin to twist wildly in the wind. Your friends are floating farther away, pursued by the creature, and you're falling behind! You'd better figure out another tactic.

Head back to 222 ●

You shuffle over toward the statue sticking out of the sand, thinking that it might offer some sort of clue as to where to go next and how to get there. Shortly you're standing before the monument, which juts out of the ground at an odd angle and is nearly covered by a dune. You brush the drifts of sand away and soon reveal the likenesses of the Ernesto Cousins! The metal of the statue has been corroded over time by the salty air of the Serendipity Sea, but the visages of Ernesto and Miguel, the heroic woodworking *primos* from East LA who found their way into the Dandelion Kingdom and saved it

from evil not once, but TWICE, are unmistakable. But the neglect and disregard this beachfront tribute has endured is more than a little sad and melancholy. What happened here? Why is everything in the Dandelion Kingdom so messed up? It's a mystery, that's for sure.

You notice that the faces on the statues are gazing in the direction of the Serendipity Sea and, if you follow their gaze, that they're looking toward the island across the waves. That confirms it—you're meant to somehow make the journey there. But how? With one last look at the sad statues, you go back to the closed gate to the Groovy Gardens. Choose another action.

Head back to 201 ●●●●

●

Using your feline reflexes, honed by years of training with Cat-Man, you tumble forward just as a chandelier shatters on the floor of the hallway! You have survived being crushed in a conflagration!

Head to 63 ●●●

●●

You juke to the left, and Dracula follows you, not allowing you to flank him that way. His lips pull back, and he bares his fangs. Do something else!

Head back to 70 ●●●●

●●●

Moving away from the crab creature, you back up against the wall of the beach hut, morbidly fascinated by the way the crazed crustacean tries to turn itself over. Even though it's on its back, it still manages to size you up and smile like it knows something you don't.

Head back to 104 ●●

●●●●

You turn and walk out the door, into the hallway. As you do, the door starts to creak—it's moving, pushed by some unseen force! Before you can react, it slams shut behind you! You grab the brass handles and try to open it, but no matter how hard you shake it, it will not move. Your only choice is to explore the hallway.

Head to 141 ●●●●

●

You stalk over to Frankenwrestler's body and STOMP on its chest. It responds by groaning in pain and rolling away. You stomp on it again and again, but it manages to roll away from your assault and lies groaning in the corner. Try another move!

Head back to 258 ● ● ● ●

● ●

Moving quickly to the right, you nearly crash into one of the other cars in front of you, which would have sent you both careering off the road. Fortunately, you both recover, but you still have to figure out a better course of action. Try again.

Head back to 5 ● ●

● ● ●

You leap toward the flames in front of you and perform a spectacular vault over them, doing the splits as you arc through the air, feeling the heat on your backside as you do! Hot dog, you've made it through the hallway and to the exit!

Head to 171 ● ● ●

The passage before you is long and dark, lined by stone and dimly lit by a row of thickly cobwebbed chandeliers that hang from the ceiling above. You can't help but think of the fire hazard the dusty webs and candles pose to everything around you, but you realize that getting out of the castle and back to the Midnight Arcade should be your first priority, not fire safety. You flex your muscles and know it's time to try to find your way home—the darkness of the corridor is ahead of you, the locked door behind. What's your next move?

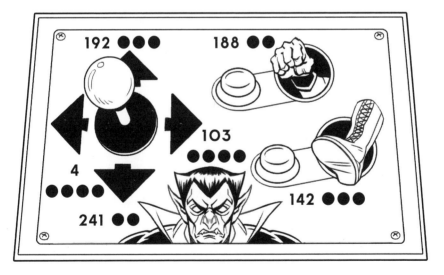

192 ●●●
188 ●●
103 ●●●●
4 ●●●●
142 ●●●
241 ●●

●

Shifting your weight to the left, you try to pull El Hombre Lobo down, but he's too strong! Attempt another move.

Head back to 14 ●●

●●

Your handsaw slices the empty space before you—*ZING!*—and you could almost swear that it cut the air itself, but how is that possible? Perhaps it was an optical illusion, but yow, that thing is SHARP. From the looks of the Groovy Gardens, with its overgrowth probably hiding all sorts of weird and strange monsters, it'll most certainly come in handy soon.

Head back to 197 ●

●●●

There is nothing here to perform a cool wrestling jump or kick on, so you don't. Instead, choose another action.

Head back to 141 ●●●●

••••

Deciding that the best way to deal with a horrific giant spider is to deal with it head-on, you flex your fingers and move forward to grapple with it. The creature moves forward as well, propelling itself through the air with its eight powerful legs, directly toward your face! Reacting with champ-like reflexes, you grab two of the legs and spin around, tossing the spider back. It hisses and crawls back toward you. Try another move!

Head back to 92 ●●●

●

You run to the right but some sort of tidal pull keeps you from moving very far. You'll have to try something else.

Head back to 167 ●●●

●●

The bridge you're on is too narrow, and you can't go that way. You can only go forward. Quick—do something else before you end up a part of the gate!

Head back to 238 ●

●●●

You approach the TV, apprehensive yet undeniably curious. You can't help but be attracted by its hypnotic glow. The Wrestling Watching Hermit is right—the picture quality IS something else!

The scene depicted on the screen has switched, though. Instead of showing some sort of weird commercial from who knows where, all you can see is what looks like a corridor in an old and musty castle—DRACULA'S CASTLE! Somehow, you're seeing inside the lair of the fiend himself. Shocked, you try to back away, but some mysterious force holds you close, and you feel as if you're being drawn toward the screen.

"Don't worry, Champ!" the Wrestling Watching Hermit says. You can see that he's holding some sort of remote control, his thumb hovering over a big red button. "I told you the Selectra-Vision Colormatic is magic, and this is one of the cool tricks it does. It WARPS you to where you need to go, and it looks like you've got a date at Drac's place. Good luck, and have fun wrestling in the castle!"

The Wrestling Watching Hermit presses the button, and the screen GLOWS. Something begins to pull on your body, a great and powerful force that draws you INTO

THE SCREEN! This is nothing like how you entered the game from the Midnight Arcade. The world goes white as you're sucked into the TV Warp, and for a moment it feels as if you're being violently turned inside out, your body twisted into ten different dimensions, and then . . .

. . . *BAM!* You are no longer in the studio hut in the haunted forest. You are instead inside the castle, and judging from a glance out a nearby window, at the top of a tall tower. The lightning storm is still raging outside. Ahead of you is a large wooden door, and you can hear the buzzing sound of electrical devices coming from beyond, like sound effects from an old horror movie. Behind you, a spiral staircase winds downward. What just happened?

"Hey, Champ!" says the Wrestling Watching Hermit in answer to your unvoiced question, his voice echoing in the chamber. You look around, expecting to see him standing there, but his disembodied voice is actually coming from everywhere and nowhere at once. "I'm not there, dude. I'm watching you on my TV! The Selectra-Vision Colormatic warped you into the castle, past those stairs! I think if you head through that door in front of you, your next match awaits!"

You reach out for the handle on the door . . . and it

opens, almost as if it was expecting you! Blinding light comes from beyond the threshold, and the hair on your arms stands up, reacting to the electricity in the air. Gritting your teeth, you can hear the Wrestling Watching Hermit one last time.

"Totally gnarly!"

And with that, you enter!

Head to 48 ●

●●●●

Deciding to go for it, you put the pedal to the metal and accelerate, heading directly toward the bumper of the car ahead of you. You get closer, closer . . . *BAM!* The front end of your car crunches into the rear end of the Ernesto puppet car ahead of you, causing it to spin out wildly and crash into the rails on the side of the road. Awesome! One enemy down, another one to go!

Head to 23 ●●

●

You cautiously move toward El Hombre Lobo, curious as to whether your opponent is faking an injury, but your hesitation costs you, as the werewolf growls and groggily gets back to his feet, his arms open and ready to wrestle again! Return to the beginning of the fight.

Head back to 171 ●●●

●●

You move farther into the garden, following the path and leaving the village behind. Soon, you're surrounded by mist behind you and walls of vegetation on either side. There's no going back now!

Head to 228 ●●●

●●●

You try to pull Dracula's arms from your neck, but he's just too strong. Your blows are useless, but you understand that before you lose consciousness. Try something else.

Head back to 34 ●●●●

●●●●

You try to avoid the Stormy by moving to the right and letting it pass, but the bad weather won't be tricked by your shenanigans! The cloud of wind, lightning, and rain envelops you, buffeting you with chilly breezes, freezing rain, and shocking electricity all at once. Let's face it, kid . . .

YOU ARE DEAD. CONTINUE: Y/N?
Y: Head to 106 ● N: Head to 265 ●●●

●

You attempt to move to the side and avoid the falling ring of candle-death, but there isn't enough space on either side of the corridor. The chandelier falls . . . directly on top of your head, and . . .

YOU ARE DEAD. CONTINUE: Y/N?
Y: Head to 125 ●● N: Head to 265 ●●●●

Your ride toward Ernestopia is proceeding without incident, and you begin to wonder if it could actually be this easy. You were expecting a race, and you've gotten a joyride through some beautiful country. But then you hear a noise coming from somewhere behind you. Turning, you see that two more cars are on the road, flashing their lights at you and gaining rapidly.

Seconds later, the cars have caught up to you, flanking you on either side. Both of the cars look almost exactly like yours, but with letters painted on the front, and the drivers . . . well, they're wooden! And they look just like the Ernesto Cousins, but twisted and weird. Mean. Almost EVIL.

For a moment they match your pace, and then both of them pull ahead rapidly, the one on the left staying in its lane and the one on the right pulling ahead of you . . . and then something falls from its trunk—it's a bunch of nails, and you're headed right toward them! What's your next move?

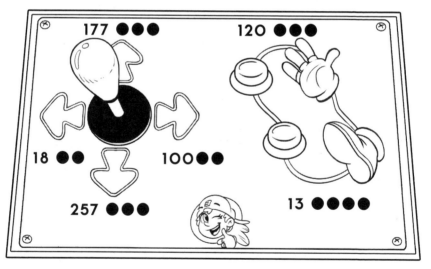

A dead end. You made the wrong choice, and it's cost you . . . your life!

YOU ARE DEAD. CONTINUE: Y/N?

Y: Head to 63 ●●● **N: Head to 265** ●●●●

You run to the right when the crab creature lunges toward you, but it's only confused by your evasion for a split second. It starts to pursue you around the little beach hut, and you can feel its crabby breath on your heels. Gross. Try another move!

Head back to 12 ●●●

●

You circle to the right of Frankenwrestler's body, for some reason deciding not to press your advantage. Is it sympathy you feel for your former friend . . . or friends? Regardless, you're not sure what to do.

Head back to 258 ●●●●

Enraged and enflamed, Frankenwrestler rises to its feet and begins to move wildly about the ring, sweeping its arms at you, but it's blinded by flame, and you easily avoid its attack. Missing you, it charges at the walls of the cage . . . and with its strength, breaks through! It proceeds to run amok around the laboratory, destroying machinery in its blind rage. Then it pounds on one of the laboratory walls, breaking through that, as well, and creating an opening! For a moment, it teeters on the precipice . . . and then falls in, disappearing from view!

You rush over to the new exit to see where Boris and Elsa have gone and peer into the hole they made—it's a long shaft that seems almost endless. You can see no sign of your opponent. You've won another match in Wrestlevania!

But now what? You've defeated El Hombre Lobo. You've watched Boris and Elsa—Frankenwrestler—plummet to their doom, but you know that you must still defeat the local champion: DRACULA! But how?

As if in answer to your unspoken question, you hear someone clear his throat behind you. Spinning around in alarm, you see that you are not alone—a small man stands there, carrying yet another torch. He's dressed in rough black clothes and has a rope tied around his waist, and his face is cruel and misshapen. It's a hunchback, and he's come for YOU!

"My master sends his congratulations on your victory," he says, beckoning to you to follow him. "He invites you to join him in the crypts below the castle for one last contest . . . against him!"

The hunchback has arrived at another section of the laboratory wall, a smooth length of undisturbed stone. "Do you accept his challenge?"

You nod grimly.

"Goooooood," says the hunchback. "You didn't have a choice! Ha-ha-ha!" He touches a hidden button on the wall, and a secret door opens, which leads to a darkened staircase. The hunchback descends the stairs and then turns back to you.

"Walk this way," he says. And you do. You walk that way and follow the hunchback down, down, down . . .

The hunchback leads you down an ever-winding set of stairs, going deeper and deeper and deeper into the lower depths of Dracula's castle, and you wonder if it would be too much for what looks to be an ultra-rich vampire lord to install an elevator. Finally, you arrive at the base of the stairwell, which dead-ends at two massive doors framed by a huge stone arch. Each door has a fearsome iron knocker in its center, shaped like a bat with its fangs bared.

"The master awaits," says the hunchback as he walks to the door on the left, raises the knocker, and brings it down once, twice, three times, each blow echoing ominously in the chamber.

Then . . . silence. A dread silence, full of unspoken terror. What's about to happen? The doors begin to rumble and move inward, dust falling from their hinges, until they are fully open. Beyond them is complete and total darkness. A chill, noisome wind blows out of the darkened chamber, causing the hunchback's torch to flicker. He smiles at you eerily.

The hunchback hobbles forward and touches his torch to a standing light, which sets off a chain reaction: Lights begin to flicker on beyond the archway, torches that illuminate a long path, lighting up one by one, their flames spreading until you can see that what lies beyond the doors is nothing short of a vast underground crypt with a WRESTLING RING at its center, a ring that the hunchback crawls into underneath the lowest rope. A microphone lowers from somewhere in the darkness above the ring, and the hunchback grabs it and begins to speak.

"Living, dead, and everyone somewhere in between, welcome to . . ."

"WRESTLEVANIA—ROUND THREE!" he bellows.

An explosion of fireworks follows this announcement, and what was once a house of the dead comes ironically alive, as the residents of Dracula's castle emerge to witness the creepy contest. Ghosts pass through walls, vampires emerge from their coffins, ghouls dig their way out of their tombs, and soon the entire hellish arena is filled to capacity with monsters hungry to see a real show.

"This is the final round of Wrestlevania, boys and ghouls, the brawl to take it all!

"Making their way to the ring now is our challenger, the hell-bound human some people call . . . the CHAMP! Give it up!"

Music begins to blast from the arena's speakers, and you recognize it as your trademark entrance music. Dracula's done his research. Knowing your cue when you hear it, you begin walking down the aisle toward the ring, accompanied by a chorus of unearthly, literal "BOO!"s from the phantoms, spooks, vampires, and other angry fans that line the route. But you know how to handle hostile crowds, whether they're angry electricians in Duluth or bloodthirsty creatures of the night in Transylvania—you hold your head up proudly, flex your muscles, and sneer right back at your detractors. You're number one, and you let them know it.

But you notice that the crowd is getting more and more unruly; the legions of the dead begin to claw at you from either side. They don't seem to want to wait for the final match—they want to BE the final match! And your suspicions are confirmed when a vampire wearing a "Dracula is #1" trucker hat breaks ranks from the crowd and leaps in front of you, hissing evilly and blocking your way.

But you continue your promenade down the aisle and

are inundated by a rain of terrifying trash as the angry, riled-up wrestling audience shows its support of ITS champion, Dracula! Thirty-two-ounce cups of blood soda bonk you in the head, and popcorn boxes filled with worms, bits of brains, and other disgusting and monstrous snacks strike you in the chest. It's a mess, and it's all you can do to keep moving toward the ring, which is now mere feet away. What do you do?

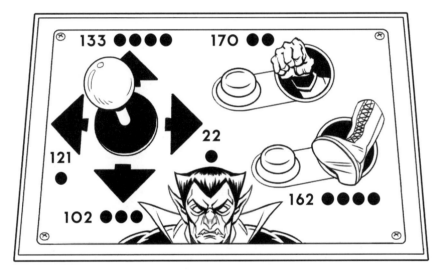

133 ●●●●   170 ●●

22 ●

121 ●

162 ●●●●

102 ●●●

●●●

Your wooden car accelerates forward, and the buzz saw disc flies after you, getting closer . . . and closer . . . and closer! You press your foot down as hard as you can, hoping to get one last burst of energy . . . and it works! You outpace the projectile, and it falls down to the road, then veers off wildly, rolling around in a wide arc before shooting off to the side. You can see your rival shaking its wooden fist in frustration as you pull away. There's no way it can catch up to you now. Cool beans! You're almost at your destination!

Head to 238 ●

●●●●

Deciding to teach these jerks a lesson, you leap up and balance on the barrier between you and the crowd and begin to kick the creeps in their heads. But as satisfying as it is to stomp on some vampire noggins, that wasn't your goal here. You're soon overwhelmed by them, and they pull you down into their ranks! You took a few of them with you, but . . .

YOU ARE DEAD. CONTINUE: Y/N?
Y: Head to 154 ●● N: Head to 265 ●●●●

Congratulations!

You got THE TORCH!

And not a moment too soon, for you see now that you are SURROUNDED by giant spiders—they're in front of you AND behind you! They approach rapidly, and you instinctually wave the torch at them in defense, which works— for the moment. The ugly arachnids recoil from the heat and fire, hesitating before they attack. The cobwebs in this section of the stairwell are thick, and you're holding the spiders at bay, but they look ready to attack any second. What's your next move?

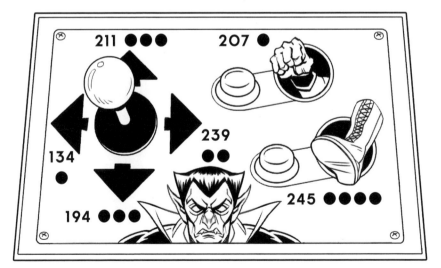

211 ●●●

207 ●

239 ●●

134 ●

245 ●●●●

194 ●●●

● ●

That does absolutely nothing. There's time for two things in this life: time to wrestle and time not to wrestle. This is the latter, not the former. Choose again.

Head back to 25 ● ●

● ● ●

You decide that the best way is just to keep running, and you do so . . . directly into the empty space in the path. You're still moving fast, but now you're gaining speed vertically instead of horizontally and . . .

YOU ARE DEAD. CONTINUE: Y/N?
Y: Head to 106 ● N: Head to 265 ● ● ● ●

● ● ● ●

You creep around El Hombre Lobo to the right as the creature groggily raises himself to his full height. You had a chance to attack again, but you missed it. What kind of champ are you, anyway? Start again, amateur!

Head back to 171 ● ● ●

●

You jump . . . and just barely make it across the gap, once again tumbling to the ground! Amazing work, but the Stormy is still behind you, and a mere gap in a floating path in the sky isn't going to stop it—it's FLOATING, for Ernesto's sake. And it's GAINING on you!

Head to 119 ●●

●●

You're running forward, racking your brain for an idea about exactly how to get through the boarded-up barrier ahead of you, when it hits you: You're in a game, you're a carpenter, and you're carrying what is probably a magic saw! Hoping you're right (and hoping you can time it correctly), you barrel toward the wood, and at the last moment, you bring the saw down and . . . *BZZZZZ!* It saws through the wood like a hot saw through wood made out of butter! Amazing! A moment later you break through the rest of the weakened wood . . .

. . . and fall! What? What a rip-off! The game is cheating! But that's when you realize you're not so much falling as you are SLIDING—the pathway has turned into a corkscrewing slide, like at a playground, but made out of smooth wood. Ha! You're alive! And no splinters . . . yet.

Looking up, you can see the angry Stormy above, furious that you've gotten away. It doesn't seem to be able to descend with you, and as you accelerate down the slide, you wonder where you're going to end up next.

Soon, your question is answered, as the slide comes to an abrupt end . . . quite a few feet off the ground! You squawk in fear, but you tumble to the ground unharmed. Looking around, you see that you are at what appears to be the exit of the Groovy Gardens, a small area dominated by a stone wall and iron gate, both of which are covered by vines. Behind you is an overgrown path back into the Gardens, and nearby there's another open paving stone.

Head to 254 ●●

●●●

You've moved even farther down the path, huffing and puffing inside your diving suit. The alarm from your air gauge is sounding again, over and over, urgently informing you that you are almost out of air. You need to find the surface and get out of the Serendipity Sea IMMEDIATELY. Luckily, you see the undersea path is actually sloping upward, and looking up you can see light coming from above—you're near the surface!

Forging ahead, you make one last dash in the hopes that you can make it. But just then, a shadow passes over you, blocking the light from above—it's the Noctopus again! Your jump last time seems to have only temporarily incapacitated the monster, and now it's back for you and has once again set itself in front of you, determined to prevent you from reaching land. You've got one chance to get past it—what do you do?

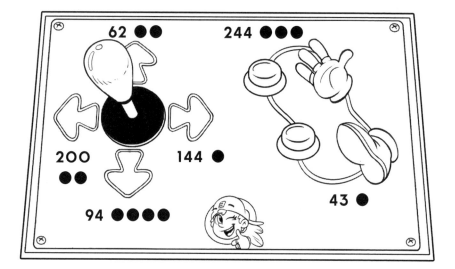

●●●●

"Vhat happened to my Transylvania Tvist?! It alvays vorks on the zombies and demons that I spar against! No vun has ever been able to break that hold before! You shall pay for this insolence . . . vith your blood!"

You've really gotten ol' Drac riled up, because now he's zooming right at you! What's your next move?

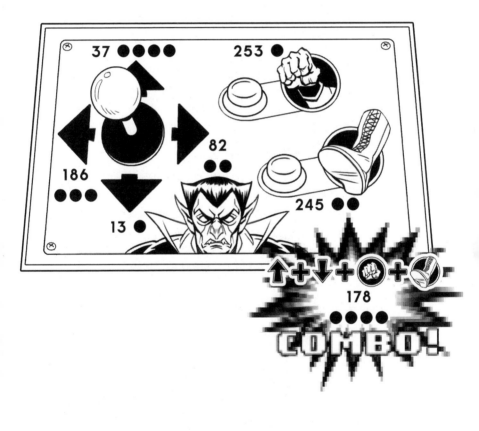

●

What does an Excellent Ernesto Cousin do when they need to take care of some wood? They use their trusty saw, that's what they do! You don't bother simply pressing the button; you punch it repeatedly, and a group of buzz saw blades shoot from your grille in response. The whirling hail of blades connects with the gate, and the air is filled with a sound not unlike that of a busy sawmill. A cloud of sawdust rises, and you roll directly into it . . . and through it! Your action destroyed the gate, and you roll into Ernestopia. That's a carpentry job well done, young cousin.

Head to 88 ●●●●

●●

Another crazed and monstrous fan jumps over the barrier and runs toward you, but you quickly smack them aside and into the crowd. But the rest of the audience is getting restless for wrestling. You need to get to the ring, and soon! Pick another action.

Head back to 154 ●●

●●●

Your leap over the fallen chandelier has taken you through the door at the end of the passage, and you're now outside the castle. You look back to see that the way you came is now consumed with flames, a burning conflagration that you escaped just in time. You now stand at the edge of the wood that surrounds the cursed place. A path leads deeper into the wood, and from somewhere down the path ahead you hear something . . . It's a wolf's howl! Scared (but curious), you walk toward the source of the ominous bellow.

Shortly, you come into a clearing in the woods, but there's something decidedly different and unnatural about it—the clearing is almost perfectly square for one thing, with four large trees at what would be its corners, and all four sides of the square clearing are demarcated by three thick, twisting vine ropes that curl around the trunk of each tree. It's strange, but that's not the strangest feature of this place, for in one of the corners there is a man, his wrists in manacles chained to a metal ring driven into the trunk of the tree behind him. And even though this man's head is bowed, he looks *familiar* to you. He groggily raises his head, and you can see that he's wearing a mask . . . the mask of a luchador! It's him!

It's your friend, El Hombre Lobo. He survived his leap
from the plane!

You move closer and begin to pull at his chains, desperate to free him, but he shakes his head in panic. He looks up at you, his eyes wild and crazed behind his mask. There's something . . . not right here.

"No, Champ. Stay away. Go far from here! It is not safe, and I am . . . not well."

He looks down, and you follow his gaze. On the side of his chest you can see a bite wound, no longer bleeding, but still vicious-looking.

"Yes, I survived the parachute jump, but when I landed, I was chased through the woods by . . ."

The night is pierced by the sound of far-off howling.

"Yes. *Un lobo*. My namesake. And I . . . I fought it off, but . . . in the struggle, the beast bit me. I passed out and woke up here—in chains!"

Looking up slowly, you can see that the clouds are moving on and that a bright full moon hangs in the sky, bathing the clearing—and you and El Hombre Lobo—in an unearthly but theatrical glow, almost like the arc lights of an arena.

"Now I am different. *Un hombre cambiado*."

Your eyes widen in understanding, and you begin to back away from your friend, who has begun to thrash back and forth, pulling at his chains.

Hair begins to sprout from El Hombre Lobo's skin, and his face beneath the mask begins to shift and warp. His eyes have turned yellow, his nose elongates like a snout, and his teeth have grown sharp and fierce. He looks like a wolf! But also . . . a man! He is now truly El Hombre Lobo. He is . . . A MANWOLF!

With one terrific burst of energy, the transformed El Hombre Lobo pulls at his chains . . . and breaks them apart! Confronted by this terrible beast, you move backward cautiously. Your first instinct is to exit the clearing and flee, but vines have twisted across the entrance of the clearing, cutting off your escape. Looking around, it hits you: You're in a weird, arboreal WRESTLING RING! This is all part of that fiend Dracula's evil plan, and your only way out is to grapple your friend . . . and win.

Your match against El Hombre Lobo has begun, and he looks more ferocious than ever before. What's your next move?

●●●●

You rush forward as Frankenwrestler throws the slab directly toward you, and it knocks you flat, pinning you to the mat and stunning you so badly that you can't defend yourself when Frankenwrestler follows up with a stunning diving elbow drop, breaking both the slab . . . and you.

YOU ARE DEAD. CONTINUE: Y/N?
Y: Head to 48 ● N: Head to 265 ●●●●

●

Deciding that you have no choice but to try to break through, you keep running, cross your arms over your face, and brace for impact . . . and *BAM!* You collide with the boards and bounce back. You couldn't break through, and now the Stormy has finally caught up with you, raining on your head, whipping your hair around with its wind, and zapping you with bolts of lightning. Guess what! That's right!

YOU ARE DEAD. CONTINUE: Y/N?
Y: Head to 119 ●● N: Head to 265 ●●●●

●●

You leap backward just as the chandelier above tumbles to the ground, splintering into pieces and blocking your way with a bonfire of chandelier rubble. Unfortunately, the way behind is ALSO covered with a bonfire of chandelier rubble. You have no path to escape, and . . .

YOU ARE DEAD. CONTINUE: Y/N?
Y: Head to 125 ●● N: Head to 265 ●●●●

●●●

You remain in the middle lane and end up driving over the nails spread out over the road. Your car starts to wobble and shake—the nails have embedded themselves into your wooden wheels, making it impossible for you to hold the little car steady. Losing control, you begin to spin out, and then your car slides off the road . . . and slams into the barriers on the side! Your license has been revoked because now . . .

YOU ARE DEAD. CONTINUE: Y/N?
Y: Head to 150 ●● N: Head to 265 ●●●●

●●●●

Thinking that now might be the right time to unleash the Wooden Stake on your opponent, you run forward and climb up the nearest turnbuckle, leap into the air, and then turn your body so that you are coming down toward Dracula with both your elbows and your knees . . .

. . . and hit the mat where he USED to be. Dracula has rolled over and evaded the Wooden Stake! You've staked too soon, and now you're going to pay the ultimate price, as Dracula quickly rises to his feet and leaps upon you, pinning you to the ground while at the same time biting your neck! Champ, it was a good run, but . . .

YOU ARE DEAD. CONTINUE: Y/N?
Y: Head to 169 ●●●● **N:** Head to 265 ●●●●

●

You turn the wheel to the left, and your car drifts a lane over in that direction. You turn it back, and you return to the center lane. Test out the other controls or . . .

**To test out the other controls,
head back to 182 ●●●**

To continue on, head to 150 ●●

●●

You creep closer to the fire, feeling its warmth on your wrestling-suit-clad body, but there's nothing here save for flames and the faint smell of dirt and the burnt something you smelled before . . . the scent of *nosferatu*—the vampires! Go in another direction.

Head back to 58 ●●●●

●●●

Feeling a little apprehensive, you try to retreat and head back toward the village, but you walk directly into a wall of fog. For a moment, you can't see anything, but then you emerge from the mist and are once again facing the path ahead. You can't go back, at least not now! Try again.

Head back to 197 ●

••••

You push El Hombre Lobo away, rush backward to the vine ropes, and use them to hurtle your body toward your opponent! As you get closer, you attempt to take the werewolf down with a flying kick, but he grabs your ankle while you're in midair, twirls you around a couple of times, and then THROWS you into the nearest tree! This match is OVER, and . . .

YOU ARE DEAD. CONTINUE: Y/N?
Y: Head to 14 ●● N: Head to 265 ●●●●

•

While running, you swing your saw behind you, hoping to cut the Stormy in two, but all that accomplishes is to provide your enemy with a lightning rod to attract its bolts. One shoots through the blade of the saw, down your arm, and into your body, and . . .

YOU ARE DEAD. CONTINUE: Y/N?
Y: Head to 106 ● N: Head to 265 ●●●●

●●

There's no opponent near to punch or grapple with, but there IS a rip cord to pull, so, figuring that your first priority in this strange situation is to stay alive, you grab the handle and yank on it. Your chute deploys in an instant, slowing you down rapidly. The wind picks up and begins to blow you around like a leaf, and it's all you can do to hold on to the straps of your parachute as you float down to the ground below. Within moments, you emerge from the low cloud cover and see that you're dropping directly into a stand of tall pine trees! Before you crash into them, you glance toward the horizon and see something amazing: There's a castle not too far off in the distance!

An honest-to-goodness Gothic castle! But your amazement is short-lived, as just then you drop into the trees, crashing through limbs before coming to a sudden stop just above the ground. Exhausted, you lose consciousness . . .

Head to 58 ●●●●

Soon, you come to the edge of the beach, which strangely enough is what appears to be . . . a parking lot? In an *Excellent Ernesto Cousins* game? Weird. But not as weird as what else is there, for the parking lot has one occupant: A tiny convertible car is parked near its exit, which looks like nothing less than the starting gate of a racetrack. The gate leads to a road that winds off toward the semblance of a city far off in the distance. Too far off to walk, at least. Aha! Hence the car!

You dash over to the small vehicle and you see that it's actually made entirely out of WOOD, from its tires to its steering wheel.

A small logo is carved on the side of the car. When you peer closer, you can see that it reads "Ernesto." Another thing made by the mysteriously missing cousins, obviously. It's actually pretty neat, and figuring that no one around here will care that you don't have your license, you hop into its snug little driver's seat. It feels . . . cute. Agile, like it'll be fun to zip along in. Next to the steering wheel you see a green button that says "Start" and you reach out to press it. *VROOM!* The engine in the little car comes alive, and the vehicle vibrates happily. There's something magical about it; it feels like it was MEANT to be driven, and you figure that you might as well give it what it wants. You press your foot down on the accelerator, and the engine revs higher. Then, you turn the wheel back and forth and feel the wheels move, and press your foot on the brake pedal. Everything checks out. That settled, you put the car in gear, and when you do, the archway above the parking lot lights up, revealing a sign that reads:

Under the archway, a red light illuminates, then another, and then another beside it glows green. Knowing your cue, you press the gas pedal and peel out, steering the car in the direction of the city in the distance. The race is on!

Though it curves and dips, the three-lane road ahead is completely clear on either side of you; but you know it probably won't be for long, so before you meet anything on the road, you decide to see what the car can do.

Let's take a test drive:

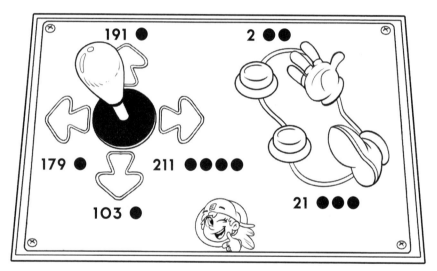

●●●●

You and the remaining Ernesto puppet car are neck and neck on the road, your cars each trying to edge out the other and get the upper hand. You're back in the middle lane, and the other car is to your right, when the other driver jerks to their left and grinds their car against yours, pushing you over toward the left-hand side of the road. It's car against car in a show of brute wooden-auto strength. What's your next move?

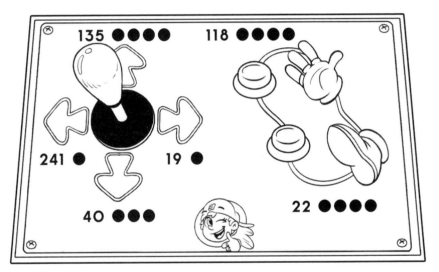

135 ●●●●   118 ●●●●

241 ●   19 ●

40 ●●●

22 ●●●●

●

You try to break free by dragging Dracula forward, but his grip is stronger than iron! And then . . . he bites you! As the blood begins to drain from your body, you think, *I should have never snuck into that dang arcade . . .*

YOU ARE DEAD. CONTINUE: Y/N?
Y: Head to 34 ●●●● N: Head to 265 ●●●●

●●

The Dandies won't let you go through them. Instead, they all bow to you, as if you were some sort of sacred personage. You can't go this way.

Head back to 75 ●●●●

●●●

As Dracula rushes your way, you move to the left and let him pass by harmlessly. He's really angry now, and he comes back around for another go! Choose another move.

Head back to 169 ●●●●

You draw the saw from your belt, spinning it around in your fingers easily, like it's a pencil in homeroom and not serrated metal meant to separate wood into pieces. *Just like an Ernesto Cousin*, you think. And then you *SLAM* the blade of the saw into the ground, ripping a great tear in the earth and sending a shock wave through the assembled crowd of Dandies. They stare at you for a moment . . . then cheer wildly!

Head to 96 ●●●●

●

You turn to retrace your steps and are immediately surrounded by the mist, which is thick, impenetrable. After a few moments of near panic and not being able to see even a foot ahead, you emerge from the mystical fog bank . . . back where you started, facing the corridor of green! Choose another direction.

Head back to 228 ●●●

●●

Your fingers try to clutch empty air, but there's nothing to grapple with here. You sense movement, though, as though something is stirring. Soon. Very soon. You can feel it (metaphorically). Pick again.

Head back to 141 ●●●●

●●●

Sproing! Nice jump, cousin. Very jumpy. But what purpose does it serve? None, at least at the moment. Do something else.

Head back to 201 ●●●●

EXCELLENT ERNESTO EXPLAINS

You place the two coins you picked up into the tray and slam it home, causing the Ernesto automaton to do a weird, jerky little arm dance in wooden robotic delight.

"TWO coins! Not bad, not bad at all! Not the best, but now it shows that you're a bit daring and not afraid to take some risks. Well, you asked for it, so here you go: Long ago, my cousin and I came to this land, the Dandelion Kingdom, and had many adventures, saving princesses and princes and, in the process, saving the land itself. Then we'd come back and do it all again, slightly the same way, but with a little variation. It was fun, sure, but after a few times, it kind of became like a job, and we already had good jobs as carpenters.

"So after a few times going back and forth between the world of the Dandies and ours, we figured out something: Instead of being participants in the game, we could use our carpentry skills to MAKE the game. So that's what we did. We retreated to this deserted island and began to craft our own sequel to our adventures, just to see if we could. And we spent YEARS doing it—heck, you saw only a fraction of the stuff we built. There's enough stuff out there to make *Excellent Ernesto Cousins 4, 5, 6* . . . I could keep going! But I won't, because you grabbed only two coins. Sorry!"

With that, the automaton abruptly stops and powers down, as if someone pulled its plug. Rats. Just when the story was getting interesting. But you won't hear the rest of it anytime soon, for now you feel your entire body begin to tingle—you're being transported out of *Excellent Ernesto Cousins 3*!

If you want to play *Wrestlevania* now, head to 126 ●●●●

If you've beaten this game and *Wrestlevania*, head to 265 ●●●●

If you want to play again later, come back anytime. You have infinite continues!

●

You hold the steering wheel steady with your hands at ten o'clock and two o'clock, and your little car stays in its lane.

To test out the other controls, head back to 182 ●●●

To continue on, head to 150 ●●

●●

You can't go that way! It's a wall! And this wasting of time has cost you, as the flames ahead of you and behind rapidly encroach on your position, and . . .

YOU ARE DEAD. CONTINUE: Y/N?
Y: Head to 63 ●●● N: Head to 265 ●●●●

●●●

You begin to walk down the hall and into the darkness, following the passage's curves until you can no longer see the door behind you. As you do, a chill breeze blows from somewhere ahead of you, causing the chandeliers above to sway and the flames on the candles to flicker. The breeze must be coming from somewhere, so you figure that there must be an exit in this direction and continue on.

Head to 66 ●●●

●●●●

You swing your saw at the crab creature, but the tool has no effect on the monster, save knocking it back a few inches and causing it to pause in a daze for a moment before it rushes back toward you. Try again!

Head back to 12 ●●●

●

Moving to the left, you deftly dodge the thrown slab, enraging Frankenwrestler. Good move, but you'll have to figure out how to actually DEFEAT the beast soon!

Head to 33 ●●

●●

You think back to the portraits you saw in the corridor of the castle and decide to try the special move that you learned there, but there's something wrong—you can't seem to remember how to do it! And this momentary confusion becomes an eternal mistake, as your special-move misfire gives Frankenwrestler enough time to throw the slab at you and CRUSH you! Oops.

YOU ARE DEAD. CONTINUE: Y/N?
Y: Head to 48 ● **N: Head to 265** ●●●●

●●●

On this side of the great room are cobweb-covered bookshelves that groan under the weight of old, moldy books that look like they haven't been read in centuries. It appears that Dracula isn't a big reader. Tsk. Choose again.

Head back to 58 ●●●●

●●●●

That way lies the trackless nothingness of the Serendipity Sea, and you will surely be chased down by the Noctopus in seconds. Try something else.

Head back to 132 ●●●

●

You move farther down the hallway just as another chandelier falls behind you. That was close!

Head to 125 ●●

You jump—*SPROING*—but your jump is much slower, and the *SPROING*y sound is muffled by the water. You land with a soft thud on the seafloor, but nothing happens. You still need to pick a different move.

Head back to 259 ●●

●●●

You back away from the spiders ahead, waving the torch in front of you as you do. They stay just out of the flame's reach, but you've forgotten that there are spiders behind you, as well. You whirl around rapidly and swing the flame at them, and they retreat, too. They're not going to let you get away that easily, so try something else.

Head back to 163 ●

●●●●

You start to circle to your right, and El Hombre Lobo does the opposite. You are stalking each other, trying to identify each other's weaknesses, neither willing to attack first. Try something else.

Head back to 171 ●●●

●

There's nothing over here except for bushes, bushes, and more bushes, thick and impassable. This is not the way. Try again.

Head back to 197 ●

●●

You spread your arms and legs in an attempt to slow your descent, and it works, kind of—you're slowing down; but you can't fly, so you'd better think of another option before you lose track of the other wrestlers or you smack into the side of a mountain, whichever comes first. Choose another option!

Head back to 222 ●

●●●

You creep closer to the creep on the mat, thinking that maybe he's playing vampire possum and luring you into a trap . . . and as you get within arm's reach, you find out that you're CORRECT, as Dracula lashes out at you, catches your ankle, and pulls you forward, causing you to fall to the mat alongside him! You turn to him and see his face glowing with hunger, and then he rolls over and PINS you to the mat!

What happens next, well, let's just leave it at . . .

YOU ARE DEAD. CONTINUE: Y/N?
Y: Head to 64 ●●●● **N: Head to 265** ●●●●

●●●●

You move to the left and promptly fall off the platform. You could have predicted this, right?

YOU ARE DEAD. CONTINUE: Y/N?
Y: Head to 242 ●●●● **N: Head to 265** ●●●●

You have left the village and entered a new land beyond it. Grass grows in the cracks between the bricks of the wide, winding path underneath your feet, and the sides of the path are overgrown with weeds and nasty-looking vegetation. The Dandies used to take care of this place, but it looks like it's been years since anyone has bothered to do some maintenance out here. *This place is busted.* Ahead of you lies the path that leads farther into the mist, and you can still hear the *Excellent Ernesto Cousins* theme on the wind. What's your next move?

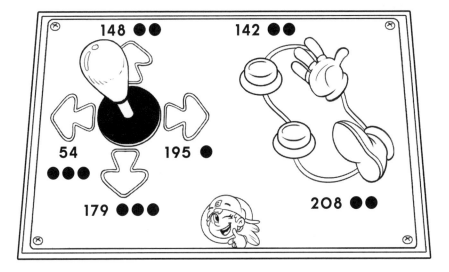

148 ●●

142 ●●

54 ●●●

195 ●

179 ●●●

208 ●●

●●

As Frankenwrestler charges you, you use its rage against it. When it's upon you, you grab both of its hands and fall backward, placing a foot against its chest and using its momentum to send it flying with both heads over heels and into one of the Tesla coil turnbuckles! The impact sets off a shower of sparks! The power fails—you've short-circuited the system!

Head to 258 ●●●●

●●●

You crouch and then leap . . . at least six feet straight up! It's impossible, but you don't feel the slightest bit odd about what you've done. It feels . . . as if you were an Ernesto Cousin. The assembled Dandies, however, are more than impressed, and they all bow and scrape as if in worship. What. The. Heck? Try another action.

Head back to 75 ●●●●

●●●●

You do a combination jump/kick, and it's good that you do, for your foot comes into contact with a chandelier that was falling toward you, shattering it into pieces.

Head to 125 ●●

You've taken down El Hombre Lobo with a suplex, and now your lupine opponent is a supine opponent! The beast lays stunned on the mat. What's your next move, Champ?

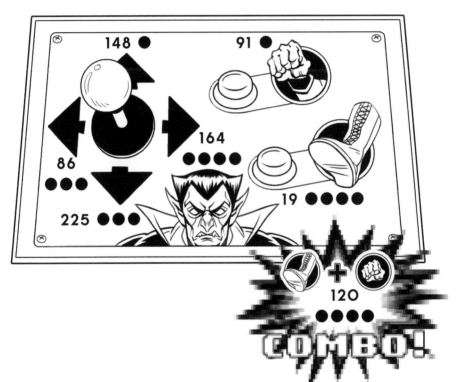

You continue running, but cut to the left at the last moment, hoping to weave around the Noctopus. Unfortunately, it slams its tentacles down in front of you, preventing you from going farther. You try to change course, but just then you get another alert from your air gauge. It's telling you that you're out of air and out of time. Basically it's saying . . .

YOU ARE DEAD. CONTINUE: Y/N?
Y: Head to 167 ●●● N: Head to 265 ●●●●

You quickly move to pin the vampire, jumping up and slamming down on top of him, shaking the entire ring! Dracula writhes and attempts to bite you, but you stay well out of his fang range. The hunchback lurches over to you and smacks the mat with an open palm.

"One!" says the hunchback as Dracula struggles beneath you. The vampire has been weakened, though, and he cannot break your hold.

"Two!" says the hunchback, and Dracula struggles again, marshaling his strength until the fiend frees himself from your grasp. This wasn't the right move!

Head back to 70 ●●●●

●●●●

To your left, down the beach a ways, you can see some sort of statue sticking out of the sand. To the right, there's a wrecked little beach hut. Ahead of you, across a short strip of sand, is the Serendipity Sea, and squinting at the horizon, you can just barely make out something in the distance . . . It's an island! That's where you need to go. But it's MILES away. What's your next move?

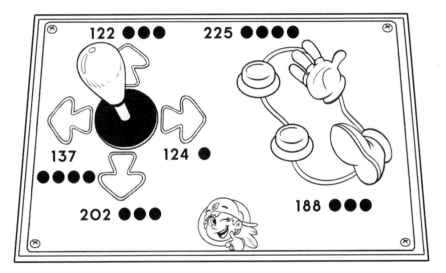

●

You pull your wheel to the right and fall in line behind the Ernesto puppet car, both of you just narrowly avoiding falling into the pothole. The race goes on!

Head to 185 ●●●●

●●

You raise the speargun and pull the trigger, and its projectile flies away into the kelp forests of the Serendipity Sea. This thing will be useful later, but for now, you'd better get moving. Your air gauge says you're running low! Choose another action.

Head back to 259 ●●

●●●

You try to turn around and go back through the gate to the garden, but the doors are shut tight. There's no going back to the Groovy Gardens—you must continue forward! Choose another action.

Head back to 201 ●●●●

You observe Frankenwrestler, lying on the ground, feeling that this might be the time to finish it off. Glancing over to one side of the ring, a lightbulb turns on over your head, or rather, a TORCH, for you see, just outside the ring, another torch placed in a sconce in the wall. That's it—the special move is TORCH AND PITCHFORK! You reach between the now unelectrified bars of the cage, grab the torch, and with it in hand, you climb upon the Tesla coil turnbuckle nearest the Frankenwrestler. Crossing your fingers, you jump from the top of it and SLAM the torch down on the body of Boris and Elsa, which ignites!

Head to 154 ●●

●

As you walk to the right from your starting point, you notice bits and pieces of the crab monster you defeated in the beach hut. But as you ponder your victory, you must forget where you were headed, because now you are back at the Noctopus Crossing sign. Try a different tactic.

Head back to 259 ●●

●●

One of the Ernesto puppet cars is in your sights, so you figure that now is as good a time as any to use your buzz saw weapon. When you press the button, a blade shoots from your grille, aimed directly at the other racer. It only takes a moment to reach them and then—*BZZZ!*—saws the car ahead of you in half! You smash through the pieces and keep going. You're in this race to win it!

Head to 23 ●●

●●●

Your handsaw slices the empty space before you. Though the air is definitely thinner this high up and seems to react differently to your action, nothing happens. Choose again.

Head back to 242 ●●●●

●●●●

Remembering the special move seemingly tied to Dracula, you steel yourself and figure that maybe you should open up with your strongest asset.

You try performing the special move, but you can immediately sense that Dracula was expecting it. He has clearly been watching you. He moves quickly out of your way and you must try again.

Head back to 70 ●●●●

●

You hit the brakes, hard, which means the buzz saw cuts into your car a lot sooner than it would have normally. It also means that the Ernesto puppet's car rear-ends yours, causing both of your vehicles to go up in a wooden blaze of glory. You had to go, but so did they, and . . .

YOU ARE DEAD. CONTINUE: Y/N?
Y: Head to 7 ● **N: Head to 265** ●●●●

You shoot a bolt from your speargun while running toward the Noctopus, and the projectile heads directly toward its eyes . . . and then gets batted away, caught by a tentacle. That didn't work. Try another action!

Head back to 132 ●●●

●●●

You move to the left, thinking you might be able to maneuver around the cars, but the car on the left decelerates rapidly as the car on the right moves over to block you. You'll have to try something else.

Head back to 5 ●●

●●●●

You decide to pass the chests by and continue down the underwater pathway, bouncing along and hoping that the Noctopus won't come back anytime soon.

Head to 167 ●●●

You thrust the torch in front of you, jabbing it at the creatures, and they dance away from the fire. They HATE this, you realize, and you do it again, eventually striking one of the spiders with the flame. It catches immediately, turning into an eight-legged, crazed ball of fire, running to and fro, igniting the bodies of the other spiders too unlucky to flee, and soon the stairwell is filled with the stench of barbecued spider.

The smell reminds you of the boardwalk and a hot dog stand you had passed earlier in the day. Your stomach rumbles. Spider meat. Disgusting, but awesome!

Head to 47 ●

●●

You leap into the air, a sprightly action accompanied by a jaunty, *sproingy* sound effect that comes seemingly from nowhere. Nice! You recall that jumping on enemies and other things plays an important part in *EEC* games and file that information away for future use. Now try something else.

Head back to 197 ●

●●●

Try as you might, you can't overcome El Hombre Lobo's lycanthropic strength, and he resists your attempts to drag him across the ring. You need to try something else!

Head back to 14 ●●

●●●●

The Noctopus's tentacles come slamming down toward you, but you manage to evade them with a quick roll to the left. But choose another action, fast! It's coming for you!

Head back to 39 ●

Feeling pulled toward the chest on your left, you rush over to it. After a quick examination, you can see that it has the name "Ernesto" carved into its face in ornate letters. You also see that the chest is unlocked! You lift the lid . . . and inside is a solitary silver coin. You grab the treasure, and when you do, the chest shimmers and fades away into nothingness as text appears in the air—no, water.

CONGRATULATIONS!
YOU FOUND . . .

ONE OF THE
SILVER COINS!

Maybe grabbing the coin will pay off later, but for now you need to MOVE. Your oxygen is running out!

Head to 167 ●●●

●●

The air is slashed by your saw, but there's nothing in front of you to separate into two pieces.

Head back to 228 ●●●

●●●

You creep up the stairs toward the spiders before you, and they skitter away from the flame in your hands. They don't retreat entirely—they still look hungry for wrestler flesh—but they definitely don't like the fire. What else can you do?

Head back to 163 ●

●●●●

You turn the wheel to the right, and your car drifts a lane over in that direction. You turn it back and return to the center lane. Test out the other controls or . . .

To test out the other controls, head back to 182 ●●●

To continue on, head to 150 ●●

Deciding that while you're down in this creepy sewer you might as well explore it all, you forgo the exit to the surface and skulk deeper into the underground. The frog sound gets louder—*ribbit*—and louder—*RIBBIT*—until you're sure that you're headed directly toward some sort of Frog City or something. Preparing yourself for the worst, you hold your saw tightly, ready to strike out at any deadly amphibians that call this place home.

As you continue on, the tunnel opens up into a large chamber. It's cavernous, actually, and three other tunnels, one directly ahead and two others to your left and right, drain into it. Above the chamber is a dome, decorated with a colorful mosaic that appears to depict the major events of the previous two *Excellent Ernesto* games in 8-bit tilework. Bizarre.

But that's not the most bizarre part of this chamber, for in its center on a wooden throne set on a raised dais, there sits a huge anthropomorphic wooden FROG dressed in a tattered robe of royalty, wearing a silver crown. It emits a loud bellow of a ribbit—this is where the sound was coming from! Well, you know what to do now. Raising your magic saw, you yell the battle cry you know all too well—"Ernesto Cousins!"—and charge

across the chamber toward the Frog Boss. But the weird carved amphibian raises both of its wooden webbed hands, as if to say, "Hey, back off, carpenter. I come in frog peace." You pause, accepting what seems to be the Frog Boss's preemptive surrender. Seeing that you're not about to start cutting it into pieces, the Frog Boss reaches up and takes off its crown and then brings its hands together, apparently crushing the piece of jewelry. But no, the Frog Boss is doing something with it, moving its hands around, shaping the crown into something else. Finally finished, it holds out what it has made, offering it to you: In the palm of its hand is a solitary silver coin. Reaching out, you gingerly accept the gift.

CONGRATULATIONS!
YOU FOUND . . .

ONE OF THE
SILVER COINS!

You've found one of the secrets of *Excellent Ernesto Cousins 3*! The coin now in your possession (still warm from whatever transformative magic the wooden creature performed on it), the Frog Boss sits on its throne and gives you a thumbs-up. Funny: You were expecting a fight, but it seems to have been expecting you, waiting to give you this strange gift. How about that?

Then, the Frog Boss waves at you, like it's saying goodbye or dismissing you. You wave back, and then you hear a rumbling coming from the other three tunnels. Suddenly jets of water shoot out of each of them, rapidly filling the chamber and buffeting you to and fro, pushing you back down the corridor you came through! You can barely keep your head above water, and when the tide pushes you past the pipe to the surface, you reach out, desperate to get a handhold on the ladder . . . and you just barely grab one of the rungs! Holding tight to your coin, you pull yourself up until you're above the raging waters. Phew. That was scary. Pausing to catch your breath for a moment, you proceed to climb up toward the surface.

Head to 254 ●●

••

This is it. The moment of truth. You know it. The time is right to drive a wrestling stake through the heart of Dracula, Lord of the Undead! You leap forward and ascend the ropes nearest to the vampire, jump off, and propel yourself into the sky, then turn in midair and pull your elbows and knees together, heading straight toward your opponent, who hisses as if you were the dawn sun shining down on him.

"Not that vun! No! Not the—"

BOOM! Before Dracula can finish his sentence, you drive your knees and elbows into where the heart would be on his chest! He screams in agony but doesn't get up. You roll over and pin him as the hunchback comes to your side and begins his count.

"One!" cries the hunchback, and when he does, it's followed by the sound of thunder and a distant cackle of "Ah-ha-ha-ha-ha!" Dracula shape-shifts in an attempt to wiggle free of your hold, his body moving from protean form to protean form, but you hold fast against his struggles.

"Two!" yells the hunchback as you continue to pin the Lord of Vampires. Another rumble of thunder echoes the countdown, and another echoing chant of "Ah-ha-

ha-ha!" can be heard, this time seemingly coming from everywhere and nowhere all at once. Dracula snaps at you with his fangs, but his teeth find no purchase in your muscle-bound flesh.

"Three!" screams the hunchback as he smacks the canvas of the ring with his open palm, and this time the thunder and the cry of "Ah-ha-ha-ha-ha!" are deafening and shake the infernal arena. You release your hold on the King of the Undead and back away quickly. Dracula rises from his prone position, standing and glowering at you with a hatred that eclipses any sports rivalry in history, his red eyes burning with bloodlust. He steps toward you . . .

. . . and ages ten years!

He takes ANOTHER step toward you, points at you with a clawed finger, and ages TWENTY years!

And he takes yet ANOTHER step, and his skin begins to crack and turn into brittle, paperlike flakes. He's now aged what seems like A HUNDRED years, and as he tries to come closer to you, he begins to break into pieces, and something within his chest starts to glow. Bloodred light leaks from his mouth, his eyes. His fanged teeth are bared, but he ages yet AGAIN, and now his whole body is crumbling and turning to dust before your very eyes. The glow from within him turns into an inferno, and his body IGNITES—*fwoosh!*—consuming him in an instant, until he's nothing more than a pile of ash in the middle of the ring. The referee approaches you, raises your hand, and announces, "The winner and STILL champeen . . . the CHAMP!"

A victory bell begins to ring, and the assembled ghouls, ghosts, and goblins in the audience go wild, their strange, ghastly cries raised in cheers for you, the winner of *WRESTLEVANIA!*

As you bask in the adulation of the creepy crowd, you feel yourself lifted up in the air by multiple hands. Looking down, you see that those hands belong to— what video-game sorcery is THIS?!—your friends and wrestling colleagues, El Hombre Lobo, Boris, and Elsa! You can't believe it, but here they are, restored back to their old selves now that Dracula's wrestling evil has been vanquished.

But that's not the last surprise of the evening, for from your perch you can see that a new creature is approaching the ring. It's a slow-moving, foot-dragging zombie, and it's carrying something in its outstretched zombie arms. The decaying corpse hits the side of the ring and, in its mindless, undead confusion, cannot get into the ring until other monsters help it up, breaking off one of its arms in the process.

One limb lighter but still carrying its burden, it continues its slow walk, heading directly toward YOU. Your friends set you down, all four of you getting into position, ready to suplex this sinister shambler. But as it gets closer and then stops in front of you, you realize that the thing it's carrying is a BELT, and it's trying to hand it to you. Cautiously, you take it, and your wrestling friends crowd around you as you take in the details of the item: It's wide and heavy, dominated by a huge golden buckle, an image of a crown in the middle, and the words "Transylvania Federation of Wrestling" written on the back in raised Gothic lettering. It's a new championship belt! You take the trophy from the zombie and smile. You're a pro, so you know what to do with this: You raise it above your head and show it to the crowd, which erupts in unearthly celebration. Then you strut around the ring, keeping the belt aloft and showing it off to every corner of the arena, because that's what a champion DOES.

So: The Dark Prince of the Night has been defeated, you have been reunited with your friends, and not only have you retained your old championship belt, you've gained a new one. *Wrestlevania* has come to a close, and you are the victor. What's your next move?

If you want to play *Excellent Ernesto Cousins 3* now, head to 75 ●●●●

If you've beaten this game and *Excellent Ernesto Cousins 3*, head to 265 ●●●●

If you want to play again later, come back anytime. You have infinite continues!

●●●

The crab creature defeated, you wipe its insides off your Excellent Ernesto Cousins uniform, trying to clean up as best as you can. Finally somewhat satisfied (but not totally free of crab slime), you return to the chest cautiously and peer inside, hoping that there isn't another one of those monsters waiting for you inside. You needn't have worried, for there's nothing in there except for an old-fashioned diving suit and a speargun. You were right—it's an outfit upgrade, one that not-so-subtly is pointing you in the direction of the sea! You quickly change into your new duds.

CONGRATULATIONS! YOU GOT . . .

THE DIVING SUIT AND SPEARGUN!
Head to 259 ●●

●●●●

Instead of going forward, you choose to walk back . . . directly toward the flaming inferno! That was a bad move. Too twitchy. Another chandelier falls, you are trapped, and, subsequently . . .

YOU ARE DEAD. CONTINUE: Y/N?
Y: Head to 20 ●● N: Head to 265 ●●●●

●

"C'mon, everybody!" you yell to your fellow wrestlers. "Let's bail!" Being wrestlers and not idiots, El Hombre Lobo and Boris and Elsa all follow you as you rush to the door of the plane, by which is a stack of parachutes. Hurrying, you grab one and strap it on, then help your friends with theirs. Once everybody's chutes are secure, you grab the door handle, wrench it down, and open the door. Wind and rain immediately enter the cabin, stinging your face with their intensity.

"After you, Champ!" says El Hombre Lobo.

"You first!" says Boris while Elsa nods.

You shake your head, and as El Hombre Lobo begins to protest, you grab him with your patented Champion Clinch and throw him out the door while pulling his rip cord. Boris and Elsa both rush you, but you flip over them like you are jumping off the ropes, and when they collide, you grab both of their rip cords, press your feet against their chests, and push them out the door with all your might. Once they're gone, you jump up and peer out into the storm—you can see three parachutes open in the distance. Phew. They're okay. For now. You grab the sides of the open door and prepare to jump, and as you do, you see something shocking on the fire-engulfed wing—it looks like there's someone, or someTHING, crouching on it! Whatever it is, it looks like a man in old formal dress, but it's got hairy, clawed hands, leathery WINGS sprouting from its back, and a head that looks like a fusion of human and bat! Seeing you, it bares its fangs and then leaps off the wing and begins zooming through the air . . . right toward the parachutes of your friends! Knowing that whatever the creature is up to, it can't be any good, you jump from the plane's door and aim your plummeting body toward your fellow wrestlers. As you streak through the stormy skies, an image flashes in your mind: the controls on the *Wrestlevania* machine, back in the Midnight Arcade! You know that you're somehow INSIDE a video game, so if you're going to make it back to the boardwalk, you're going to have to think like a video game player. So what's your next move?

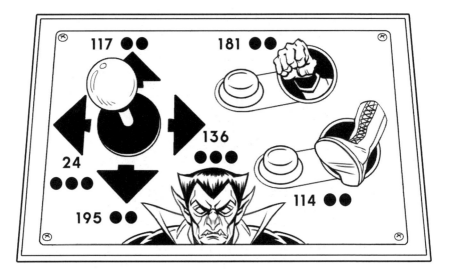

●●

Feeling a bit nervous about all of this, you try to back up and descend the way you came, but . . . there's nothing there! The mist has risen so much that it's completely obscured everything below you. You can't even see the next platform down, much less jump down to it. Choose another action.

Head back to 242 ●●●●

●●●

You back away from El Hombre Lobo, cautiously waiting before you deliver another blow, and that wariness gives him time to recover. The creature rolls over and rises, ready once again to engage! You'll have to start over!

Head back to 171 ●●●

●●●●

You use your saw on the empty air and cut it quite nicely, if ineffectively. Your weapon won't help you here . . . at least not yet. Choose another action.

Head back to 201 ●●●●

●

You stroll casually forward, directly into the inferno. It turns out that you are not fireproof. Guess what? That's right . . .

YOU ARE DEAD. CONTINUE: Y/N?
Y: Head to 63 ●●●   N: Head to 265 ●●●●

●●

You move back down the path, the way you came. After walking for what seems like several minutes, you encounter the same scene as before, with the Noctopus sign staring you back in the face. You've magically walked in a circle. Try another move!

Head back to 259 ●●

●●●

Instead of going in for the kill, you warily circle Dracula to the right, and the ancient bloodsucker takes advantage of your hesitation, using the extra time to get to his feet. You had him, and you gave up the chance to pin him, and now he's ready to go again!

Head back to 70 ●●●●

●●●●

You walk directly towards the wall where the paintings are hanging. They seem to vibrate as you get closer but nothing happens. Very exciting. Choose again.

Head back to 66 ●●●

●

You dodge to the left as the crab creature skitters forward, and it begins to chase you, claws clacking at your heels, narrowly missing your ankles each time. You can't keep this up forever. Do something else!

Head back to 12 ●●●

●●

You try to move to the left and get around the giant spider, but it quickly moves to block your way up the stairs. Think fast and act again!

Head back to 92 ●●●

●●●

As far as you can tell, the Groovy Gardens has grown wild over the years—maybe decades—since anyone has tended to it. What was once an orderly and delightful garden maze has become a wild thicket of vines, thorns, confusing cul-de-sacs, and mysterious monsters, the latter of which you can hear scooting through the green herbary. When will you meet them? Soon, probably, so you'd better make haste and get through the Groovy Gardens before you wind up as a snack.

Ahead of you, the Gardens' walls stretch farther into the depths of the Gardens. Behind you, there's a thick wall of mist. To either side of you, there's simply vegetation. But that's when you notice something weird—the floor of the garden is mostly earth, but beneath your feet is a large round stone that looks almost like a manhole cover for a sewer. It even has little holes drilled in it for drainage. Dead plants and old dirt obscure what looks to be something written upon the lid. Kneeling down, you brush them away to reveal a strange motto etched into the stone.

OVER OR
UNDER OR
STRAIGHT ON
THROUGH,

WHATEVER
• DIRECTION IS •
UP TO YOU.

That's weird. What could it possibly mean? Perhaps
you'll solve the mystery somewhere along the line, but
for now, what's your next move?

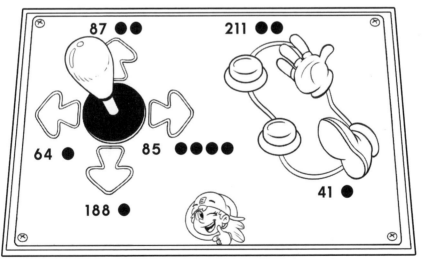

87 ●●   211 ●●

64 ●   85 ●●●●

188 ●   41 ●

EXCELLENT ERNESTO EXPLAINS

The mechanical Ernesto waits patiently, but when it becomes apparent that you have nothing for it, it sighs.

"Oh well," it says, its jaws clicking. "Looks like you won't be getting any answers. Goodbye!"

And with that, you feel your body start to disintegrate, turning from digital data back into physical data. You've managed to make it to the end of *Excellent Ernesto Cousins 3* alive, but you didn't learn any secrets. What a rip-off!

If you want to play *Wrestlevania* now, head to 126 ●●●●

If you've beaten this game and *Wrestlevania*, head to 265 ●●●●

If you want to play again later, come back anytime. You have infinite continues!

●

As your eyes adjust to the darkness, you notice that you're at the beginning of what looks to be a network of stone tunnels underneath the Groovy Gardens. Above you, roots from the garden have begun to break through cracks in the stone. Ahead, the tunnel stretches off into darkness. Flashlight in one hand, saw in the other, it's time for you to decide: What's your next move?

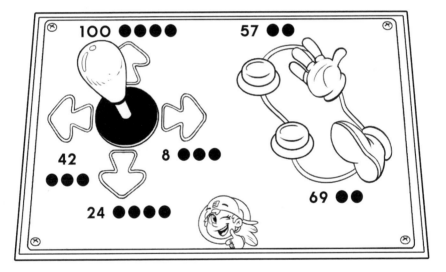

●●

Terrified, you turn and try to flee back down the stairs, only to run into a freshly spun web a few steps down. It ensnares you, and as you struggle to break away from its stickiness, you get hopelessly entangled. The harder you try to get free, the more trapped you become, and that, unfortunately, gives the spider time to catch up to you . . . along with a few of its friends. Face it . . .

YOU ARE DEAD. CONTINUE: Y/N?
Y: Head to 92 ●●● N: Turn to 265 ●●●●

●●●

You cautiously creep closer to inspect the prone, double-headed body of what used to be the greatest tag team in the world. It seems to be down for the count, completely unconscious, so you lean down to take its pulse—there's nothing there. You've won! But your celebration is short-lived, for you've forgotten one thing—it was already dead. Frankenwrestler's eyes—all four of them on both heads—open, and its hand grabs your wrist. It was a trick, a dirty trick! It quickly grabs you with its other hand, stands, lifts you over its head, and then brings your body down over its knee for a vicious backbreaker. OUCH.

You will have to be more cautious the next time you are checking the pulse of your undead opponent. You've lost this match, Champ. But maybe if you're lucky, Dracula will use the same technique he tried on Boris and Elsa, bring you back to life, and use you as an undead sparring partner. At any rate . . .

YOU ARE DEAD. CONTINUE: Y/N?
Y: Head to 258 ●●●● N: Turn to 265 ●●●●

EXCELLENT ERNESTO EXPLAINS

You count out the three coins you found and carefully place them one by one into the coin tray. Once placed, you drive the tray home, and the machine practically roars to life, its mechanical eyes opening wide and its head turning around a full 360 degrees.

"Wow, wow, wow! THREE coins! You did it! You beat my game! And yes, I mean MY game. Or rather, I should say OUR game, for my cousin and I built everything around you. Yes, we made Ernestopia. This entire world is our creation, in fact. Here's the deal: Long ago, my cousin and I came to this land, the Dandelion Kingdom, and had many adventures, saving princesses and princes and, in the process, saving the land itself. Then we'd come back and do it all again, slightly the same way, but with a little variation. It was fun, sure, but after a few times, it kind of became like a job, and we already had good jobs as carpenters.

"So after a few times going back and forth between the world of the Dandies and ours, we figured out something: Instead of being participants in the game, we could use our carpentry skills to MAKE the game. So that's what we did. We retreated to this deserted island and began to craft our own sequel to our adventures, just to see if we could. And we spent YEARS doing it—heck, you only saw a fraction of the stuff we built. There's enough stuff out there to make *Excellent Ernesto Cousins 4, 5, 6* . . . almost infinite games. We spent years building things and hoped that one day someone would come along—a long-lost cousin, you see—to help us run the Dandelion Kingdom. But we got lost in our work, neglecting the Dandies in their village, ultimately becoming legends to them. You've met them. Strange characters, huh? But after some time, my cousin simply got tired of the whole rigmarole and went home. I stayed behind and worked, ol' Hermit Ernesto, but then I decided to split, too. So I built this, my final contraption, and spread the coins around the Dandelion Kingdom so someone could unlock my message. Now the game is over. The Dandies should be getting word by now that the Ernesto Cousins have left the building, and that they shouldn't wait up for us anymore. They'll receive a sign. How? Check this out . . ."

The Ernesto automaton trails off, slowly stopping its movements. You pound on the glass again, but there's no response. It has spoken its last sentence.

Huh. That's it?

But then, you feel a rumbling shaking the ground, as if something—something huge—is crawling up through the dirt from deep beneath the earth. The rumbling intensifies until you're sure Ernestopia is undergoing a massive earthquake, a trembler that you might not survive. And then you realize that the disturbance isn't coming from below, it's coming from the huge statues, which aren't statues at all—they're actually Excellent Ernesto automatons, just like the drivers of the cars and the automaton in the box, but crazy big! They stride toward you, their motions almost comically slow, and when they're almost upon you, they look down . . . and salute! Then, they both begin striding away, stepping over the walls of Ernestopia (the ones that haven't fallen down, at least), and walk in the direction of the beach. Soon, the wooden golems are gone from view, and you stand there, stunned. They'll probably walk through the Serendipity Sea, after which they'll make their way to the Groovy Gardens and, ultimately, the village of the Dandies, who are in for a pretty big shock. The Dandies are going to FREAK. OUT.

Wow.

What a WEIRD game.

Those Ernesto Cousins sure liked making wooden tributes to themselves, and they sure seemed to get a kick out of messing with the heads of the Dandies.

What a WEIRD ending.

And now that you've uncovered the game's strange secret, you feel yourself being transformed, being pulled back to the Midnight Arcade. You've beaten *Excellent Ernesto Cousins 3*, so now what?

If you want to play *Wrestlevania* now, head to 126 ●●●●

If you've beaten this game and *Wrestlevania*, head to 265 ●●●●

If you want to play again later, come back anytime. You have infinite continues!

You are at last alone on the road, your final adversary dealt with, and you're rapidly approaching the city limits of Ernestopia. You can see now that it's not a glimmering city but a grand village, built entirely out of wood, and surrounded by a tall fence, like an old fort. But something isn't right—the road ahead leads to a narrow bridge that takes you to the entrance to Ernestopia, and the end of the bridge is blocked by a stout wooden gate that is closed! Think fast, cousin!

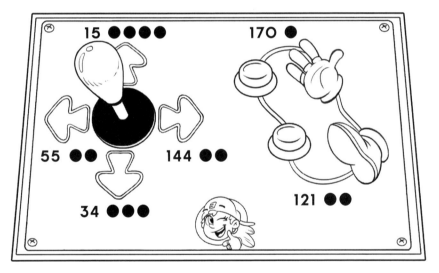

●●

Gingerly, you creep to your right. You notice that they don't seem to be concerned that you're trying to get away from them, which you find odd, but you're not going to question their motives. You move slowly, and the spiders all watch you as you go . . . directly into a freshly spun web! You twist and turn, dropping the torch in panic, hoping to break free, but you only end up wrapping yourself in a web cocoon, like the stick at a cotton candy maker. Soon, you're fully wrapped, immobile. The spiders move toward you, and they couldn't look any hungrier if they were holding knives and forks and had napkins tied around their arach-necks.

YOU ARE DEAD. CONTINUE: Y/N?
Y: Head to 163 ● N: Head to 265 ●●●●

Terrified, you hit the brakes hard, causing your car to skid and slide around until you're facing backward but still sliding forward toward the pothole! You're slowing down, but not enough, and you feel your back wheels roll off the edge of the deep cut in the road, and then . . . you tip over and fall in. Your brakes, they failed.

YOU ARE DEAD. CONTINUE: Y/N?
Y: Head to 23 ●● N: Head to 265 ●●●●

●●●●

Maybe NOW is the right moment to use that special move you learned back in the corridor of falling chandeliers? Well, either way, you're going to give it a try. As Frankenwrestler barrels toward you, you leap up and try to come down on its heads with a terrific kick, but it stops you in midair, grabbing you by the throat and smiling as you feebly try to free yourself from its Frankengrip. Then, using its terrific strength, it throws you into the nearest Tesla coil turnbuckle. The impact sets off a chain reaction, shorting out the entire system and, as a sad side effect, frying you like an egg.

YOU ARE DEAD. CONTINUE: Y/N?
Y: Head to 33 ●● N: Head to 265 ●●●●

●

You turn your wheel to the left, temporarily disengaging from the car driven by the Ernesto puppet, but you're only free for a moment as the car swings back to collide with you and continues to push you toward the edge of the road. Do something else!

Head back to 185 ●●●●

●●

You can't go this way. The door is locked tight. Try as much as you like, but it won't budge.

Head back to 141 ●●●●

●●●

You begin to move to the left, slowly walking along the seabed for several minutes. As you walk you notice bits and pieces of the beach hut unceremoniously strewn about. After a couple of minutes, you have returned to the Noctopus Crossing sign as though you hadn't gone anywhere at all. Choose a different action.

Head back to 259 ●●

●●●●

You decide to ascend the floating platforms, jumping up, up, up—*sproing, sproing, sproing!*—until you are far above the Groovy Gardens. The strange mist that permeated the grounds rises with you platform by platform, until you can no longer see the ground and you're seemingly trapped in the sky.

Gulp. That doesn't seem good.

Finally, the platforms come to an end. You've reached the top, and ahead, separated from you by a void of sky and mist, is a pathway in the air that leads . . . somewhere! You can't tell exactly where, but it seems promising, at least.

So, here you are on a floating paving stone, possibly hundreds of feet in the air, and before you, across a short gap, is a strange sky road. What's your next move?

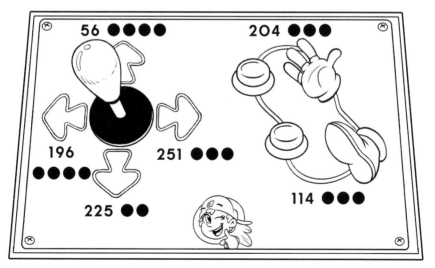

●●

Frankenwrestler throws the slab directly at you, and you valiantly attempt to use your grappling skills to grab it in midair and perform an impressive diverting move, but the thing is actually heavy. REALLY heavy. It would have looked really cool if you had succeeded, but instead you're crushed under the slab's weight, and . . .

YOU ARE DEAD. CONTINUE: Y/N?
Y: Head to 48 ● N: Head to 265 ●●●●

●●●

Here goes nothing, you think as you rush toward the Noctopus. You could swear that it's smiling at you, expecting an easy meal. But that's not your plan at all. As the last of your air is exhausted, you aim the speargun on the run . . . and fire! Your bolt whooshes through the water too quickly for the Noctopus to deflect it with a tentacle . . . and *SMACK!* It's a direct hit in the Noctopus's eye! The creature wildly thrashes back and forth in pain, and you take advantage of its confusion to slip past it and make your way to the shore as your oxygen runs out. You're getting closer, but your vision is getting darker, and darker, and darker . . . You're passing out. You're not going to make it! You're so close and . . .

. . . *splash!* You break the surface of the water! Somehow, you've made it past the Serendipity Sea. That was amazing. Give yourself a pat on the back, but before you do that, get that helmet off and take a breath of fresh air!

Head to 39 ●

●●●●

You leap into the air, attempting to squash another spider into paste with a well-placed stomp of the wrestling boot, but as you do, the flame of your torch brushes against the cobwebs that line the ceiling of the stairwell, and they almost burst into flames! You're going to need to be more careful in your combat. Pick another action!

Head back to 163 ●

●

The crab creature scuttles toward you, and you rapidly retreat and let it chase you around and around the interior of the hut. How are you going to defeat this thing? It's time to pick another action.

Head back to 12 ●●●

●●

You wait . . . wait . . . wait . . . and when Dracula is almost upon you, you sweep his leg, tripping him and sending him flying to the mat, face-first! You've turned his anger back on him, and now you've got him on the ropes, er, the ground!

Head to 64 ●●●●

●●●

You decline the Wrestling Watching Hermit's offer of getting a closer look at his weird television. It gives off a weird vibe, as if it's emanating some sort of mystic radiation. You assume that, at best, the Wrestling Watching Hermit is imagining things and that if you show any more interest, he'll keep you here forever and talk your ear off. And at the very worst, you imagine that his magical television would actually end up being a portal to a warp dimension, a portal that would probably send you to someplace even more horrible than Dracula's castle.

"Your loss," he says as you wave goodbye at his door. "You're missing out on some MUST-SEE tee-vee. But hey! Hold up one minute, Champ!" He runs back into his hut, and you can hear him rustling around inside, knocking over stacks of junk, until he returns holding a pen and a worn-looking publicity photo: It's of you, right after you won your first belt! "If you could sign this for me, I'd appreciate it."

You do so gladly, always happy to help out a fan. You turn to go, heading back to the forest and toward the castle, when the Wrestling Watching Hermit calls out one last time.

"Kick some vampire butt, Champ! I'll be watching!" You give a thumbs-up and then reenter the forest, hiking past the ring where El Hombre Lobo is still out of it. Soon, you come to the walls of the castle and see that the fire is still raging inside the passageway you exited previously. You won't be able to get access to the tower here, so you start to walk along the perimeter of the castle, looking for some other access point. As you do, the electrical storm continues to rage above you, the lightning intermittently striking the towers above as if there is some sort of force drawing the bolts there, hungry for their energy. But what could it be? You'll find out soon enough, for you have come to another entrance to the castle, an archway that leads to a spiral staircase winding upward toward the electricity-crowned tower. Feeling that this is the only way to go, you enter and begin to climb the stairs.

Head to 92 ●●●

●●●●

You decide that the best offense is a decisive one, and inspired by the weird portrait you saw in the hallway, you decide to jump into the air while delivering an elbow to El Hombre Lobo's chest, but he dodges this clumsy attack with werewolf agility, and you slam into the ground, stunned. Taking advantage of your momentary lapse of reason, your former friend leaps into the air and lands on you with a grotesquely hairy elbow. You try to get up, but the pain is too great, and the last thing you see is the toothy maw of El Hombre Lobo's face as he leaps on you. Unfortunately . . .

YOU ARE DEAD. CONTINUE: Y/N?
Y: Head to 171 ●●● N: Head to 265 ●●●●

●

You bend your knees and push off against the floor of the sea, leaving behind a cloud of disturbed sand in your wake. You're safe—for now. But your air is running out. Hurry up and choose another move!

Head back to 16 ●

There's nowhere to go in that direction, just more seaweed bushes blocking your way. Choose another action!

Head back to 132

You jump into a backward somersault and land just out of the grasp of the Noctopus's tentacles, buying yourself a moment to think of another move. But you've only got a moment—the Noctopus looks HUNGRY. Choose another move.

Head back to 39 ●

●●●●

Figuring that one good jump deserves another, you once again jump into the air—*SPROING!*—get a little hang time, then—*CRUNCH!*—land on the crab creature's belly, your feet going through its abdomen and straight through to the floor. Its claws click a couple more times, but the creature's heart isn't into it (possibly because its heart is on the bottom of your work boot). Gross. But yay!

Head to 220 ●●●

●

Normally, you'd use your hands to grab one of the paintings and break it over the head of an opponent. This time, however, you decide on a gentler course of action and, thinking that this could mean something, you use your fingers to wipe the gunk off the brass plates under the paintings, revealing the words below.

Head to 20 ●●

●●

Pressing your foot down on the brake, you decelerate slightly, and the other cars pull farther ahead of you. You can see that this isn't going to work, so you take your foot off the pedal and pick up speed. Soon, you're back at your previous position. Drive, er, differently!

Head back to 5 ●●

●●●

You decide, for some odd reason, to step off the floating platform and into the nothingness. There's no mystery here . . .

YOU ARE DEAD. CONTINUE: Y/N?
Y: Head to 242 ●●●● N: Head to 265 ●●●●

●●●●

You hope to do some nimble maneuver to bypass the boarded-up section, so you hop up onto the railing with the aim of scooching along and going around. And you almost make it! Instead of performing some sort of spectacular move, though, you slip off the railing and plummet down into the mist. That's it . . .

YOU ARE DEAD. CONTINUE: Y/N?
Y: Head to 119 ●● N: Head to 265 ●●●●

●

You advance toward El Hombre Lobo, and he charges at you! A moment later, you are locked in a fierce grapple hold, his clawed hands on your shoulders, his nails digging into your skin. You're strong, but you're still human, and his strength is powered by the full moon. This match is ON like Lon (Chaney Jr., that is)!

Head to 14 ●●

●●

You can't go back—you're going forward! Forget about that and choose another action . . . quickly!

Head back to 106 ●

●●●

You move to the right, and in its rage, Frankenwrestler misses you and heads with both heads directly into the electrified barrier of the ring. Howling from the pain of the electricity going through its body, the creature turns to face you and charges again. Try another tactic!

Head back to 33 ●●

●●●●

Terrified, you start to reverse crab-crawl up the beach, hoping to escape the reach of the Noctopus, but you're too slow—or it's too fast, or a combination of both—and its tentacles whip out before you can get too far away, wrapping tightly around your ankles. Satisfied with its catch, the Noctopus retreats back into sea, dragging you along with it. You almost made it to the next level, but instead . . .

YOU ARE DEAD. CONTINUE: Y/N?
Y: Head to 39 ● N: Head to 265 ●●●●

●

As Dracula moves directly toward you, you meet him head-on, taking his head under your arm, lifting his body up, and then falling backward. You've unleashed a NEW move, something you think you'll call the Van Helsing Suplex! You quickly roll over on top of the vampire and pin him to the mat while the hunchback rushes to your side and begins to count.

"One!" says the hunchback as you fight to keep Dracula down. The hunchback raises his hand again and is about to count two, but . . . Dracula writhes wildly and throws you off! You'll have to do better than that if you want to get the Prince of Bats to concede defeat.

Try another move!

Head back to 169 ●●●●

●●

You're back into the Groovy Gardens, but from the looks of things, you're far off from where you started. You're no longer in the maze of overgrown hedges. Now you're near a tall wall, one of the borders of the Groovy Gardens, beyond which you can hear the sound of surf—you're near an ocean! There's a gate in the wall, and it's covered by a mass of gnarly vines and rotting vegetation, blocking you from passing through. You begin to dig and cut through the mess, figuring that the only way out of here is through.

Soon, you clear enough of the lawn clippings away to have access to the gate. You push open the doors, and beyond, you can see the expanse of a beautiful beach. Moving forward, you leave the Groovy Gardens, passing through the gates into what appears to be a protected cove, beyond which is a calm and pleasant ocean. The sun is shining, the waves crash in regular, rhythmic cycles, and the sand beneath your feet is warm and inviting. Normally, you'd pause and sit down to enjoy

your magnificent surroundings, but there's something about this place that, like the garden, seems a little . . . off. It has the air of abandonment, as if this used to be a place where folks came to have fun and to frolic but hasn't been visited in a long time. Before you is a wooden sign attached to a wooden post driven deep into the sand. It reads:

But this doesn't feel serendipitous at all. The beach feels desolate, deserted, HAUNTED. That's it—haunted.

As you look about, you hear something behind you. Turning, you see the gates to the garden are closing, being moved by an unseen force. You rush toward them and try to hold them open, but whatever's pushing them is too strong for you. You dig your heels into the sand to brace yourself, but it's no use; the doors of the gate meet in the middle and lock tight. No matter how hard you pull, they won't budge. That way is impassable. You turn around and take in your surroundings.

Head to 201 ●●●●

●●●

Your car slows down, but not slow enough to avoid the trail of nails that litter your path. The pieces of metal are driven into your wooden wheels, making your car vibrate uncontrollably and causing you to swerve, slamming into the rails on the side of the road and shattering your car—and your body!

YOU ARE DEAD. CONTINUE: Y/N?
Y: Head to 150 ●● **N: Head to 265** ●●●●

Frankenwrestler lies before you, moaning in pain, immobilized temporarily, its body smoking. This could be it . . . but it could also be a trick. What's your move?

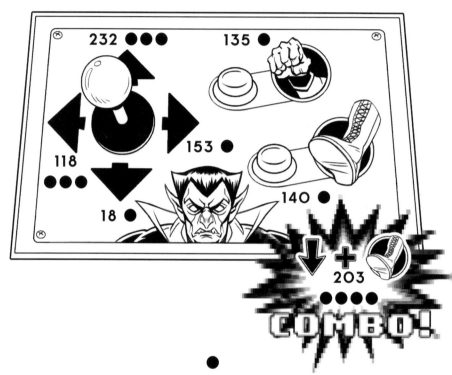

BZZZ! Nope, sorry. You're trapped in Dracula's arms. Trying this move now is nothing short of something that a button-mashing novice would attempt, a lame go-for-broke strategy that shows you aren't attuned to the finer nuances of both wrestling and gameplay. Basically what we're trying to say here is that trying to pull off a finishing special move when you're at a complete disadvantage usually doesn't work, and usually includes now. Nice try, though. Too bad that Dracula is choking the life out of you, meaning that in 3 . . . 2 . . . 1 . . .

YOU ARE DEAD. CONTINUE: Y/N?
Y: Head to 34 ●●●● N: Head to 265 ●●●●

●●

Aquatically outfitted with your saw at your belt and your newly acquired speargun in hand, you *clomp, clomp, clomp* out of the beach hut and walk toward the water. It's time to go swimming, and you are READY. You stand on the edge of the Serendipity Sea, diving suit on, taking in the beautiful view before you, the late-afternoon sunlight glinting off the gentle peaks and caps on the surface of the water. It's a pleasant scene, and you take a moment to let it sink in. *Ah*, you think, *the Serendipity Sea sure was named well.*

And that's when you see it, off on the horizon. A small swell that is rolling toward you, a swell that seems to be growing exponentially larger as it gets closer . . . and larger . . . and closer . . . and larger . . . and closer . . . until it's an ENORMOUS wave, headed right toward you!

You stand there in terror, watching the monstrous wall

of water, and then . . . *crash!* The sea consumes you
and the beach hut simultaneously. Panicking, you thrash
about as you're tossed back and forth by the wild fury
of the ocean, hoping not to drown, but then you realize
that you're actually able to breathe—you're in the diving
suit, after all. Relaxing, you pause and let the current carry
you as you slowly sink to the bottom of the Serendipity
Sea, finally coming to rest on the cloudy bottom, the
weighted boots of the suit keeping you upright. You're
also glad to notice that you've managed to hold on to
your speargun, which will probably come in handy down
here in the depths. Who knows what nautical nemeses lie
in wait in the briny deep? Knowing the *Excellent Ernesto*
games, they'll be cute *and* dangerous!

You tilt your head up and move it left and right to
get a better feel for your surroundings. Above, you can
just barely make out the surface; it's too far to swim to,
especially with the weighted boots you're wearing. Around
you is a jungle of bioluminescent underwater flora, which
gives your surroundings a cheery, if slightly eerie, vibe.
Beneath your feet and leading off into the distance ahead
are paving stones just like the ones back in the Groovy
Gardens. Figuring that you're being told something, you
start to plod ahead down the path, happy that you found

the diving suit and alert for any enemies about.

As you walk along, though, you begin to sense that you're not alone down here. Well, obviously—it's the sea, home to a variety of life-forms, and you can see an incredible assortment of weird, glowing fish and the like swimming about—but the sense you're getting is that you're not alone in a BAD way, like you're being watched. And that's when you see it: Another wooden sign is staked into the ground up ahead. Walking up to it, you see this:

You are being watch? That doesn't make sense. You feel the water move behind you, a disturbance in the current, and whip around to see a dark form cross the path from the way you came, moving from seaweed bush to seaweed bush too fast to get a good look at it. And then you see something move on your left, and then on your left again, and again, each time moving too quickly to get a good look at it! You continue along the path, looking over your shoulder warily.

Moments later, you hear a buzzing noise, like some sort of alarm. An alarm under the sea? But it's not coming from outside, it's coming from inside your helmet! That's when you notice a flashing gauge on your wrist. It's an oxygen meter, and from the looks of it, you're running perilously low on air to breathe! According to its apparently arbitrary way of measuring, you have approximately six units of air left in your tanks. You'd better hustle! What's your next move?

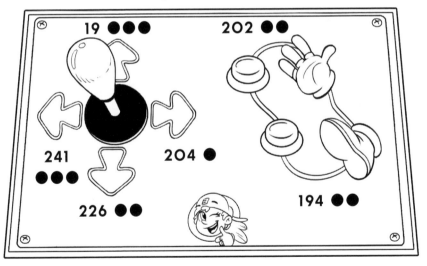

● ● ●

You slowly orbit the crab creature by moving to the right, being careful to stay out of reach of the deadly, grasping claws, which almost snag you multiple times. It's truly a sight to see, this weird monster trying as hard as it can to turn itself over and return to hunting you in the confines of this cabin. You ponder the strangeness of nature and the persistence of life, whether it's in the real world or here, in the Dandelion Kingdom, and in those pondering moments, the crab creature is coming ever closer to turning itself over and getting you in its sights. That's nature for you!

Head back to 104 ● ●

●●●●

Everything around you starts to quickly disassemble into digital noise, and you can see nothing but dancing colored lights until for a brief moment everything goes white and you're . . .

. . . out in front of the old arcade on the boardwalk, and it's completely quiet. There are no more arcade sounds and no colored lights glowing from inside. Looking through the boarded-up facade of the arcade, you can only see faint shadows of the interior. You shout, hoping to get the attention of the creepy guy who greeted you, but there's no one there. Like the rest of the San Retro Bay Boardwalk at this hour, the place is empty.

Head drooping, you start walking back the way you came along the San Retro Bay Boardwalk. *How long was I in there?* you wonder. It's still nighttime and desolate except for the rhythmic rolling of the ocean. As you walk away, you pause, still unsure about what happened, and glance back at the arcade. Still empty-looking. Still vacant. Despite everything you remember, you figure you must have had some sort of weird waking dream. You reach into your pocket to check your phone but feel something unfamiliar in there, something small, round, and metallic. When you take it out, your eyes grow wide.

It's a token from the MIDNIGHT ARCADE.

As you stare at the coin, you could swear that you can hear, far off in the distance . . . evil laughter. You turn in the direction of the sound and, for an instant, you think you see a bat's wings, or maybe a wooden bird's wings, beating far off in the sky. But the vision lasts for only a second, and when you blink in disbelief, the sky is once again dark and featureless. But you heard what you heard, and you saw what you saw.

You clutch the strange souvenir tightly in your fist and jam it back into your pocket. Ha! It WAS real, after all. Everything DID happen. As you head back toward the vacation house, you promise yourself that some night soon you'll come back here. Why? Because it's one of the rules of video gaming: A good game deserves a sequel. You smile to yourself, knowing that this is not . . . THE END.

ABOUT THE AUTHOR

Known for the popular online role-playing game *Sword & Backpack*, Gabe Soria has written several books for Penguin Young Readers, including *Regular Show's Fakespeare in the Park* and Shovel Knight's *Digger's Diary*. He has written several comic books for DC Comics, including Batman '66. Gabe also collaborated with friend Dan Auerbach of the Black Keys on the *Murder Ballads* comic book. He lives in New Orleans, Louisiana.

ABOUT THE ILLUSTRATOR

Kendall Hale is a cartoonist from Wisconsin whose work has varied from animated character designs to commercial advertising. He has produced work for Nick Jr., Bento Box, Skippy Peanut Butter, and Sandman Studios. He has also taught classes at Brigham Young University. He currently lives in Los Angeles, California, with his pet rock, Rock.

For my mini-bosses, Caleb and Felix—GS

W

PENGUIN WORKSHOP

An Imprint of Penguin Random House LLC, New York

Text copyright © 2018 by Gabe Soria. Illustrations copyright
© 2018 by Kendall Hale. All rights reserved. Previously published
in hardcover in 2018 by Penguin Workshop. This paperback edition
published in 2019 by Penguin Workshop, an imprint of Penguin Random
House LLC, New York. PENGUIN and PENGUIN WORKSHOP are trademarks of
Penguin Books Ltd, and the W colophon is a registered trademark of
Penguin Random House LLC. Printed in the USA.

Visit us online at www.penguinrandomhouse.com.

Library of Congress Control Number: 2018016070

ISBN 9780593093665

10 9 8 7 6 5 4 3 2 1